Virginia's Getting Hitched

CAROLYN ZANE

THE
BRUBAKER
BRIDES

SILHOUETTE *Romance*®

Published by Silhouette Books

America's Publisher of Contemporary Romance

For Irish "Ay-Ay" Alcalen and Richelle Louisa, from the
Philippines, my number one fans, and the Queens of my
fan club. You guys are true heroines.

And, to the Lord who commands us to love one another.
—*Galatians* 5:13

 SILHOUETTE BOOKS

ISBN 0-373-19730-6

VIRGINIA'S GETTING HITCHED

Visit Silhouette Books at www.eHarlequin.com

Printed in U.S.A.

CAROLYN ZANE

lives with her husband, Matt, and their three children in the rolling countryside near Portland, Oregon's Willamette River. Like Chevy Chase's character in the movie *Funny Farm,* Carolyn finally decided to trade in a decade of city dwelling and producing local television commercials for the quaint country life of a novelist. And, even though they have bitten off decidedly more than they can chew in the remodeling of their hundred-plus-year-old farmhouse, life is somewhat saner for her than for poor Chevy. The neighbors are friendly, the mail carrier actually stops at the box and the dog, Bob Barker, sticks close to home.

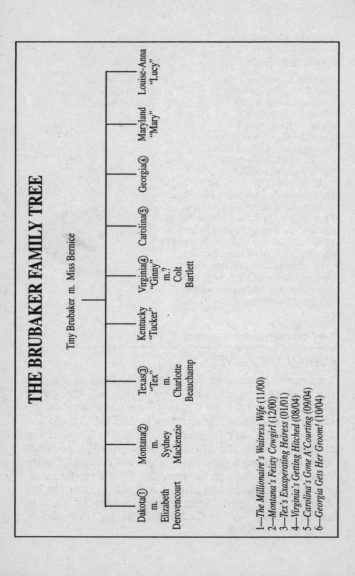

THE BRUBAKER FAMILY TREE

Tiny Brubaker m. Miss Bernice

| Dakota① m. Elizabeth Derovencourt | Montana② m. Sydney Mackenzie | Texas③ "Tex" m. Charlotte Beauchamp | Kentucky "Tucker" | Virginia④ "Ginny", m.? Colt Bartlett | Carolina⑤ | Georgia⑥ | Maryland "Mary" | Louise-Anna "Lucy" |

1—*The Millionaire's Waitress Wife* (11/00)
2—*Montana's Feisty Cowgirl* (12/00)
3—*Tex's Exasperating Heiress* (01/01)
4—*Virginia's Getting Hitched* (08/04)
5—*Carolina's Gone A'Courting* (09/04)
6—*Georgia Gets Her Groom!* (10/04)

Chapter One

"And, so, using these…uh…*scientific* methods of courting, our dear Dr. Ginny hopes to find herself a husband."

Eyes dancing, lips twitching, Virginia Brubaker's sisters struggled to maintain even a modest sense of decorum in front of their elegant aunt.

"Beg pardon?" Miss Clarise Brubaker tilted her head back and with a slight adjustment of her trifocals, studied her madly blushing niece.

"A better half."

"A superior half."

"A pedigreed half."

"A bluuuue-blooded half."

"Would you guys kindly shut *up?*" Virginia—or Ginny, as she was known by her family—cast a quelling glare at her two grinning-idiot younger siblings. But alas, rather than having the desired effect, her rancor merely had her sister Carolina slapping her thighs most indelicately and her other sister, Georgia, pinching her nose to keep the iced tea from exploding from her nostrils.

Ginny rolled her eyes. She'd kill them later. In private.

"So, ah, darlin'—" Miss Clarise's refined Southern drawl held a distinctly puzzled note. "You're hoping to rely on science rather than the heart when it comes to planning your future?"

"Sounds a bit snobbish, huh?" Ginny smiled sheepishly, and then with meticulous fingers she folded her napkin, tucked it under her plate and squinted daggers at her sisters. She could tell it was going to be a long, lo-o-ong visit. She and her sisters had only arrived at their uncle Big Daddy's Hidden Valley, Texas, ranch that afternoon and already they were testing the limits of her good humor. How would she make it through an entire summer with these two curly blond clowns?

The four women were all seated on well-padded lounge chairs under a bamboo lanai. Perched at the edge of a swimming pool, the setting was something straight out of a tropical paradise. Gentle sounds of a waterfall tumbling down a hill and into the pool mingled with those of a hot tub that bubbled magically from the middle of a rock garden. The spicy aroma of gardenias and orchids wafted on late-spring breezes. One could easily imagine that the sprawling vista unfurling beyond the lanai was an ocean of water, and not grass, the way the endless fields seemed to undulate in waves. Long purple shadows cast by the afternoon sun only enhanced this illusion.

Every summer as a child—while their parents traveled on business—Ginny and her eight brothers and sisters would come spend several weeks here, at the Circle BO, named for her uncle's famous Brubaker Oil empire.

A hint of children's laughter echoed in the back of her mind as she remembered those happy, carefree summer vacations. Eight siblings, nine cousins and a whole raft of servants' children made for some pretty spectacular high jinks and fun.

Then, one at a time, they'd all trundled off, and the summer visits began to wane. It had been a decade since she'd last spent more than a day or two here. So, when Miss Clarise recently wrote and invited her, Carolina and Georgia to come for a summer of rest and relaxation upon completion of their higher educations, well, Ginny had leaped at the chance.

Now, as she glanced at her two snickering sisters, she had to wonder why.

"It's not quite as calculating as it sounds, Miss Clarise." Ginny reached across the table to give her aunt's hand a reassuring pat. "It's just that my dissertation was entitled *The Influence of Perceived Physical Attractiveness Versus the Effects of Environment upon Selection of Love Objects*—"

Carolina and Georgia bit their lips and had to look away.

Shooting them a tight smile, Ginny forged ahead. "—where I set out to prove success and failure rates of marriages based on said selections. To make a long story short—"

"Mmm, hmm. Short. Sure," Carolina murmured into her iced tea.

"—my findings indicate overwhelming evidence that we should not choose mates based upon perceived attraction, but instead, our selections should take into consideration other, more enduring factors such as a social background that resembles our own. We 'socially validate,' so to speak, our attitudes by societal comparison—"

"In other, *English* words, Miss Clarise," Carolina interrupted, "Ginny wanted you to put in a good word for her with your neighbor's son. Brandon McGraw?"

"I did not." Ginny's rear molars ground even as she forced herself to remain serene. *I will not stoop to their level. I won't. I won't. I won't.*

"Yes, you did." Carolina turned to Georgia. "Didn't she indicate a perceived interest in the McGraw specimen?"

"I seem to remember that she mentioned he might provide a certain 'social validation,'" Georgia replied.

"I did *not!*" Had their legs not been in full view under the glass tabletop, Ginny would have added a colorful streak of black and blue to the smooth tan of both her sisters' shins. How had they managed to reduce her to a six-year-old in such record time? She was a doctor of psychology, for heaven's sake. She, of all people, should be immune to their childish goading.

"Girls, girls." Miss Clarise's gentle laughter burbled forth. "Oh, how I have missed y'all. You know, I always wanted to give my Patsy a sister or two, but Big Daddy just kept givin' me boys." She signaled a member of the household staff to clear their dishes and bring the coffee. "So, Virginia, darlin', you are feeling the urge to marry, and perhaps, settle down?"

With a wary glance at her sisters, Ginny nodded, grateful that at least her aunt understood. "My next birthday will be my thirtieth. I think it would be nice to be married for a while before I have children."

Carolina opened her mouth.

"That's lovely." Miss Clarise nudged the cream in Carolina's direction, seemingly to keep her busy as she leaned toward Ginny. "I'm so proud of you, sugar. A doctor! Why, you're the first in the family. It must be so gratifying."

"It is." Again, Ginny felt the heat flood her cheeks at the praise. Though Miss Clarise had nine children of her own, she and her husband, the lovable, diminutive Big Daddy, had always managed to make her feel special. And dearly loved.

"I'm sure you'll want to see some of your old friends very soon. Big Daddy and I are throwin' a little barbecue for you girls tomorrow night and invitin' some of your compadres from the old days. As luck would have it, I have already invited Brandon McGraw and his parents."

Lashes fluttering, Carolina and Georgia swooned at the mention of Brandon's name. Miss Clarise playfully whapped their hands.

"Y'all are excused. Go swim." Miss Clarise waved them off even as Ginny's sisters stood and bolted toward the pool house. After a genteel sip of coffee, the older woman winked at Ginny. "Honey, don't let those cheeky monkeys embarrass you about wanting to get to know Brandon McGraw. He's a lovely man. I think it's wonderful that your thoughts are turnin' to love. Big Daddy will be so tickled."

It was true. Big Daddy wanted nothing more than the members of his family to experience the passion in their own relationships that he still held for his wife. Ginny wanted that, too. Although at this point in her life, she realized that her path to that passion would need a bit of a boost from the lab.

"Miss Clarise, I've spent a lot of years building toward my career, and—" elbow to table, Ginny rested her chin in her palm and angled her head toward her aunt "—well, it's just that in my short time as a practicing psychologist, I've already seen so many marriages fail. It's really, really sad."

"Mmm." Miss Clarise nodded.

Ginny decided to come right to the point. "Anyway, I'm busy and I don't have a lot of time to waste on searching for Mr. Right, so I've decided to expedite matters with science."

"But what about love, darlin'?"

"Oh, that'll come, I'm sure. Studies show that personality type and compatibility are very important in the relational arena."

A small smile tugged at Miss Clarise's lips but she offered no comment.

"I know it sounds cold-blooded, but I'm confidant that by narrowing the available pool to men in my social sphere, and then administering a few simple tests, well… Voilà! Less time searching, more time…"

"Smoochin'?"

For the first time that afternoon, Ginny allowed herself to smile.

"I'm gonna kill you guys." Ginny slammed an empty suitcase shut, lugged it to her closet and stored it with a thud. She dusted her hands and perused the vast array of storage nooks. Perfect. Already she felt at home in the suite she'd shared with her sisters and cousin Patsy when they were kids.

Fortunately, this time around, each girl had her own private quarters, complete with a luxurious bath, gigantic walk-in closet and bedroom—with a corner

Beyond the window, the sun was hovering on the western horizon and the twilight shadows were encroaching. Off in the distance, a herd of cattle lowed as they headed to the barn for their evening milking and soulful cricket song resonated from the fields. Ginny drew a deep breath of country-fresh air.

With the exception of her noisy sisters, these were the soothing sounds of a quiet evening at home. It had been a long, tiring day of travel. She set out a pair of pajamas, as she planned on turning in early with a good book and a cup of herbal tea.

"You're *kidding!*" Carolina's delighted whoop echoed her sister's as she scrambled up to her knees and craned to see out the window. "What are they doing?"

"Basketball. Over in the driveway by the garage. Looks like a rousing game of horse. Doesn't that just bring back the memories?"

"*Yuh huh!* Let's go out there and get in on the game!"

Ginny glanced out the door to catch Carolina launching herself off the bed and out of view.

"That's a great idea," she called from the closet, relieved that they were finally leaving. "You guys go. Have fun. I'll just stay here and unpack."

"You can unpack later," Carolina snorted. "Get out here. Let's go shoot some hoops."

"Wait," Georgia ordered. "I have a better idea."

The excitement for the outdoors was suddenly replaced with the hushed whispers and giggles of a couple of prepubescent ninnies. With a weary groan, Ginny set to sorting her clothing by color and style. How would she manage to get in any relaxation this summer, with these zoo inmates swinging from the chandeliers?

It was hard to believe that they'd all come from the same womb. An amazing thing, the human psyche, she mused. How it was affected by ancestral genetic patterns, birth order, nurture, nature…

It was too quiet.

Just what in heaven's name were they up to now? Ginny craned backward to glance out the closet door. Though she couldn't see much, she could hear the sounds of a purse being dumped on her comforter and, elbows akimbo, the two frisky girls quickly pawed through its cluttered contents.

"Hey, clean that up," she called.

"We will." Their answer was distracted. Without even making a limp pretence at tidying up, they once again vanished from view. After a moment, the faucet at the wet bar turned on. Then off. Then on. Then off.

Then on again.

More giggling.

More whispering.

Okay. Something was rotten in Denmark. Ginny quickly hung a tidy row of shorts next to their matching tops, intent on getting out there and taking control.

"Here, give them to me," she heard Carolina say.

"No!" Georgia hissed. "I want to."

"I want another one. It was my idea."

"You guys knock off whatever you're up to out there. I don't want water all over my floor."

"Don't worry." Snorts, hoots and more pitter-pat of mischievous feet.

"Kenny! Hey! Kenny! And Hank! Guys, up here!"

Ginny could hear the French-paned doors leading to her veranda swing open, and from her closet vantage point she could see both of her sisters hanging over the wrought-iron balustrade, waving at their cousins and their cousins' buddy.

"Georgia! Carolina! Please!" Ginny didn't have the energy to baby-sit these dorks.

"Guys! Yoo-hoo! Up here! It's us!" Carolina yodeled. "Hi, Hank! Hi, Kenny!"

"Hey you!" Kenny's voice grew stronger as he trotted across the driveway. "Hey, guys, look! It's cousin Carolina! And Georgia! When did y'all get here?"

"This afternoon!"

"Where's Ginny?" another male voice inquired from below.

Ginny opened a satchel of shoes and paused in their organization. That low baritone was amazingly familiar. Sounded almost like…Colt? Her childhood chum, all grown up? Could it be?

Colter Bartlett? A slow grin prodded the irritation from her lips.

Good grief, she hadn't seen him in…well, *forever.* From the summer they'd come into this world to the summer they'd graduated high school and headed off to college, Colt had been her best friend. And then, for some reason, myriad reasons actually, they'd lost contact.

As she arranged her shoes at right angles, she contemplated going out and saying hello, but knew she'd never get to bed once her sisters sensed she was open to hosting a visit. Tomorrow would be soon enough for reunions. When she was fresh and tidy.

Still, it was tempting to see what he looked like.

"Colt Bartlett," she murmured. Just the sound of his name evoked such wonderful images of a carefree youth. Seemed like a lifetime ago.

Seemed like yesterday.

Like lightning bugs in the evening shadows, glowing memories flitted through her mind, in particular, the summer before fifth grade. That was the summer she and Colt had stumbled upon that abandoned clutch of duck eggs down in the reeds at the edge of a cow pond. After some discussion, they'd agreed that these babies might not hatch without help, and decided to take the eggs under their own wings, so to speak. There had been four eggs, one for each of their pockets.

Together they'd squatted among the bulrushes, making grand plans for the future of their offspring. The ducklings would surely follow them everywhere. Show-and-tell would make them stars. Maybe somebody would want to make a movie about a boy and a girl who'd hatched their own flock of ducks. They'd even picked out names....

Colt's mom and Miss Clarise had complained about the odor of rotten eggs for several days before they realized the smell was coming from their children.

A chuckle rose in her throat.

And then, there was the time they'd absconded with the riding lawn mower and accidentally decimated a patch of Miss Clarise's prize hybrid tea roses. And of course, who could forget the time they'd nearly burned down the barn during a little cigar-smoking experiment gone awry.

The disgust in Georgia's voice tore Ginny from her reverie.

"Yeah, Dr. Gin's up here, too," Georgia informed them. "Cleaning, as usual. Hey, Colt! How are ya doing?"

"Hey, girls. So, Ginny's cleaning, huh?" Colt asked. "Now?"

"Yeah." Carolina waved a dismissive hand behind her. "She's still alphabetizing her wardrobe."

Kenny snorted. "And your stuff is all over the floor already."

"Ha, he remembers!" Georgia laughed. "Come here, you guys. Let us get a good look at you!"

"Woohoo!" Carolina taunted. "Somebody's got muscles! Hankie boy's all grown up! Put your shirt back on before I forget you're my stinky little cousin."

Hank threw back his head and laughed. "Yer lookin' kinda curvy yourself, cuz."

"I *know!*" Shoulders back, Carolina preened and posed. "Who'da thought? C'mere, Kenny! You, too, Colt."

Again, curiosity tugged at Ginny's less disciplined side. Her old playmate, Colt, was right outside the window. How compelling. And, at the same time, a tad disconcerting, considering all the secrets they'd shared growing up.

Colt knew all about her mortification of shopping for her first bra. And the mortification of her first kiss with Billy Payne, the chef's son. And the mortification of five years' worth of braces. And the mortification of... well...simply everything prepubescent.

"Ginny!"

It was Colt.

"Stop stuffing shoe trees into your slippers and come out here and be sociable."

Eyebrow quirked, Ginny glanced at the shoe tree dangling from her fingertips.

So much for an evening of beauty rest. She smoothed her hair and checked her sleeveless white shirt for spots. Taking a deep breath, Ginny composed her face into her serene, fully grown Dr. Ginny facade and stepped out of the closet, only to be met with screams and shrieks coming from the veranda.

And, oddly enough, from *below* the veranda.

"What the…?" male voices sputtered with shock.

Female hilarity mingled with indignant male howls.

Carolina shouted, "Run, Georgia!" and dragged her sister through the French doors and back into the bedroom. "More balloons!"

"Get 'em!" Colt's exasperated holler echoed from below. Rails vibrating, he began his ascent up the ornate iron posts of the veranda, cousin Kenny hot on his heels. Hank scaled the rose trellis.

"No!" Georgia squealed as they reloaded. "We've got more where those came from!"

It was all so uncivilized. Her sisters were cavorting in ways that—in her professional opinion—would require years of therapy to resolve. "Carolina! Georgia! What in heaven's name do you think you are do—"

Ignoring her, the girls tiptoed out to the veranda's rail, but when a hand clamped Carolina about the ankle, they emitted high-pitched squeals that no doubt had mosquitoes dropping dead for miles. Water balloons exploded right and left. Men shouted.

"Back!" Carolina ordered, giggling.

Seeing that the boys had no intention of obeying, she turned on her heel and—grabbing Georgia—ran in giddy circles around Ginny's bed, bolting over the mattress, crawling, leaping and laughing as she flew. Three pairs of muscular arms clutched the black iron railing of her veranda. The girls screamed.

"No! Stop it at once!" Using her most authoritative voice, Ginny pointed at her sister as if this solitary digit could stop the madness.

Colt propelled himself over the railing and burst through the doors to Ginny's suite. Likewise the soaking wet Kenny and Hank—revenge in their eyes—thudded to the veranda's floor and took off after Carolina and Georgia.

"Run, Georgia! Over here! No! No, no, go back!" Carolina's frenzied orders ran afoul as she and Georgia collided then howled with crazy laughter.

Kenny grabbed Carolina and slung her over his shoulder. Hank followed suit with Georgia.

"Nooo!" they cried, but their limp protestations were more encouraging than anything.

"Put them down!" Ginny said sternly. "I mean it. You guys are dripping all over this handwoven, imported carpe—"

"Ginny, old girl, you're just as bossy as I remember," Colt told her as he grabbed her around the waist.

Helpless in his steely grip, Ginny's heart filled her throat as she found herself suddenly airborne and tossed over his shoulder like a half-filled sack of potatoes. Gracious, this was certainly not in keeping with the sophisticated impression she'd wanted to make at their reunion.

"Bu—bu—Hey!" Ginny sputtered, filled with indignation. "I didn't—I'm not—put me down! You're getting me all wet!"

"You've always been all wet."

This was the second time Dr. Ginny had been insulted in one afternoon. It was getting a little tiresome.

"Where are you taking me?" she groused as they headed out into the hallway and followed her cousins and sisters down the stairs.

"Why, out for a swim. Just like old times."

"A...*swim? Now?*"

"Why not? The evening's perfect for it."

"But—but—but—" The blood rushed to Ginny's head, making her dizzy and, as she bobbed haplessly along, she pounded on his brawny derriere. "I'm not wearing my suit!"

"Like I said. Just like old times."

Sure. Old times. When they were four and she was as flat as a tortilla, and he was as skinny.

Something had happened to her old buddy Colt, the gangly boy who'd been like a brother to her. Something wonderful and at the same time…so very…disconcerting.

This Colt was a stranger.

Oh, he was just as playful as ever, but there was something…she groped for the psychological nuances and then suddenly realized that little Colter Bartlett was a man. A powerful man with arms like steel girders and a grip like a carpenter's clamp.

A wave of melancholy glanced her thoughts. Little Colt, and her childhood, were gone for good.

Chapter Two

Colt nudged the gate to the tropical-garden area open with a hip. Still carrying Ginny over his shoulder, he ambled down the concrete deck toward the deep end of the pool. Somewhere ahead, Ginny noted churlishly as she bob, bob, bobbed along, Carolina and Georgia were having fun. Seemed Kenny and Hank had hauled them to the pool and were swinging them back and forth over the water's edge.

Stomach in her throat, Ginny clung to Colt like cellophane as he easily sidestepped their pandemonium, mounted the diving board and strode out over the dark blue water. The long springboard wobbled violently as he shifted Ginny from his shoulder and into his arms. The sun was fading and the tropical wonderland was shrouded in early evening shadows. From below, the pool's night-lights glowed eerily. Slowly, Colt moved to the very end and peered over the edge.

Ginny buried her face in his neck and squealed.

Good grief, he was *serious!*

They were serious!

Ginny's breath came in quick, frenzied little pants.

No, no, no! She didn't want to go for a swim. Not *now.* Not like this.

"Wait! These are my good shoes! This is my good watch! I just had my hair done!"

Colt grunted as he extracted her arms from his neck and held her out over the water, where she dangled in midair.

She scrambled back into his arms and clutched his shirt in her fists. "Would you just quit? This isn't amusing! This blouse is dry-clean only! I can't remember how to swim!" Ginny grasped at any old straw, hoping to convince him to let her go.

No such luck.

"Well now, I guess you should have thought of that before you bombed us with water balloons!"

"But I didn't have anything…*to do…withhhh thaaaaat!*" Screaming all the way, she followed her sisters into the pool.

Ginny gasped just before she felt herself plunge into the chilling water.

Doggonit!

This was so *unfair.*

Now, intrinsically, she knew life was never fair. After all, years of psychological study drove that point home. But still. She was being punished undeservedly. Punished for a stunt her cockamamy sisters had concocted. Just like when they were kids.

Through the roiling, bubbling water, Ginny could see her sisters thrashing about. She could hear their

muffled laughter and their shrieks of feigned indignation as they popped to the surface and splashed the
laughing men. But Ginny allowed herself to sink slowly
to the bottom, at first to avoid their flailing feet and
then…well, then she figured she'd lounge for a moment or two down near the drain and let them all wonder. As she descended past the watery light and into the
shadows, her mind began to whir.

It was payback time.

Perhaps a touch of fear would serve them all right.

After all, her hair was already ruined so what the heck.

Like auburn seaweed, her shoulder-length mane
floated lazily about her head as she descended. Remain-
ing as motionless as possible, she hovered at the pool's
bottom and watched the air pockets that had filled her
blouse and shorts burp forth in great bubbles and rise
past the light to the surface.

The water chilled her fury and she began to enjoy the
quiet serenity. In her peripheral vision, she could see her
sisters being lifted to the deck by her cousins. She
sensed they were having a bit of conversation, and,
though she couldn't discern the words, she could tell
they were discussing her. Her sisters were dismissing
her little act, but the boys seemed a tad concerned.

She smiled.

Good. Yep, yep, yep. Just a little payback.

Relaxing, she allowed her arms to rise above her
head. She figured she had another sixty seconds or so
before the jig would be up and she'd need to come up
for air. But a minute was a long time when one was
watching from the surface.

Mmm, hmm. She only wished she could see their
faces.

As she lounged under six feet of water, she was chagrined to realize that her sleeveless white cotton camp shirt was now completely translucent. Drat. Her sisters still sported their afternoon swimsuits under their shorts and tops. And here *she* was in a set of undies. How undignified.

Ah well. She had more pressing business at hand. Like the fact that her lungs were beginning to burn from lack of oxygen. What was the matter with these dolts? Were they simply going to stand there and watch her drown?

She swallowed back a bubble that had risen in her throat.

Hurry.

Hurry, hurry, hurry.

Ginny wished she'd taken a bigger gulp of air before she hit the water, but there hadn't exactly been time. Air was funny like that. Didn't really miss it till there was none. She willed someone to come to her rescue before her chest exploded.

The debate raged on at poolside. The laughter was dying and the voices had begun to argue.

The male tone of voice was urgent.

The female tone was skeptical.

Urgent.

Skeptical.

Urgent.

Silence.

Ginny rolled her eyes. For crying in the night, she'd be on the other side of the pearly gates before they sorted themselves out and came to her aid.

Moments passed.

Male and female voices began to murmur.

More moments passed.

Ginny swallowed another throat bubble and gritted her teeth. Still, no help arrived.

Okay.

The ratfinks weren't buying her act. Time to admit her ruse was a bust.

But, before she could begin her ascent, there was an explosion of bubbles overhead. Someone had plunged into the pool. Ginny felt a pair of strong arms—instinct told her it was Colt—grip her around the waist. Though she was dying for air, she forced herself to go limp in his arms. Using the coiled power in his thighs, her savior pushed off the pool's bottom and jetted them both to the surface.

As they burst into the night air, Ginny could hear her sisters' frantic voices.

"Someone call 911!" Carolina shrieked.

"Who knows CPR?" Georgia shouted.

"I do." Colt's voice was so reassuring, Ginny was tempted to forget that all this drowning stuff was simply an act.

"Bring her over here, man," Kenny instructed as he and Hank waded into the shallow end, still fully dressed, and reached to help Colt pull her out of the pool.

"She must have hit her head," Hank suggested.

"Nooo," Carolina moaned. "I never meant for it to go this far."

"I've got her. Get back." Colt clutched her to his chest, forged over to the shallow water and slogged up the pool's steps, where he carefully laid her on the concrete deck. "Somebody, get a cushion from one of those lounge chairs under the lanai."

Tearfully, Carolina rushed to comply and suddenly Ginny felt her head cradled on a thick floral pad.

"Hurry," Georgia whimpered. "Do something."

Ginny bit back a smile. *Oh, this was so good.* Uh-huh. This was worth every minute of torture she'd endured at her sisters' hands since arriving at her uncle's ranch. She ventured a teensy peek between her fluttering lashes at the concerned crowd. Kenny and Hank hovered at her feet. Her sisters knelt at her side, clutching each other in fear. Colt was busily unbuttoning her blouse.

Unbuttoning her blouse?

Good heavens. This was going a bit too far, but what could she do but lie there, limp as a freshly fished trout. His fingers burned a trail down her placket, and soon her blouse was tugged from her waistband and splayed open to reveal her lacy Wonderbra. Ginny fought an involuntary flash of embarrassment that rushed from her chest and burned in her cheeks.

How humiliating!

"Stand back and give her air," Colt commanded. "I'll start CPR."

CPR?

Oh, crap.

She gritted her teeth as Colt lifted her in his arms and crushed his mouth to hers. She tried to remain limp in his arms, but it was tough with him moving his lips over hers this way. And then there was the matter of his tongue…teasing, probing…

This was CPR?

Since *when?*

Confused, Ginny tried to go with the flow as she sorted out the information that was bombarding her senses, and automatically opened her mouth beneath his.

Good heavens, she'd taken several first-aid courses and this fancy stuff had never been part of the curriculum.

Colt's hands were roving her back, and little grunts of pleasure were escaping his throat.

Wait just a darn minute. Instead of whimpering in fear, her sisters were honking with hilarity. Kenny and Hank also seemed to be enjoying the show, if their hoots were any measure.

Ohhhh-kaaaay.

Rogue feelings of excitement warred with anger as once again they all had a good laugh at her expense. Before Colt could react, Ginny pulled him on top of her and rolled toward the pool. Indignation made her strong, and in moments they were both in the water once again. They sputtered to the surface and this time Ginny was laughing, too.

The look of surprise on Colt's mug was priceless. As were the expressions of admiration on her sisters' faces.

Okeydokey, Ginny thought with satisfaction as she shook the water out of her hair, this time *she'd* had the last laugh.

The lanai lights flashed on, and Kenny lit the tiki torches that were planted in the surrounding garden area. Since everyone was now in the mood for a swim, the men wasted no time in heading to the pool house and changing into extra swimsuits that Miss Clarise kept on hand for just such an occasion. Carolina and Georgia already wore suits from their afternoon dip, so they stayed poolside, hurriedly wiggling out of their damp clothes.

Carolina was darling in a flowered tankini and Georgia was bouncing about in—and spilling out of—a low-cut one-piece that surely would have fit her better a decade ago. Noisily, the boys emerged from the pool house bare chested and tanned, sporting brightly colored swim trunks. They torpedoed the water with gusto, causing Ginny's sisters to emit more lusty screams of joy.

Standing by herself in the shallow end, Ginny glanced down at her soggy blouse and realized that she was the only one dressed from chin to knee. She felt all at once matronly and removed from the fun. For a second, she contemplated changing into a swimsuit, but figured changing into her pajamas and calling it a night would probably be the wiser choice.

She stifled a yawn.

It had been such a long day. And now, trying to fit in with Gidget's beach party here, well, it just sounded like far too much work. As she threaded her way through the water to the ladder, Colt swam up behind her and touched her arm.

"Where you going?"

"I, uh—" Suddenly flummoxed, Ginny turned to face him, her gaze catching his before moving to her hands. That kiss, though it had been a joke, had somehow changed the way she looked at Colt. She felt awkward and a little bit shy. It was ridiculous, but feelings were feelings. No controlling those. "I thought I'd turn in for the night," she explained to the fingers that nerves had her twisting in knots. "It's been a long day."

"Ah, c'mon," Colt urged. "You can sleep all day tomorrow. You only just got here. Stay out and play with us, Scooter-pie."

The silly nickname from their childhood had Ginny grinning in spite of herself. It had been years since anyone had called her that. "But I'm not wearing a swimsuit."

"So?"

Her eyes were drawn, as if caught by a magnetic field, to Colt's, and their gazes tangled. Somewhat dizzy and disoriented, Ginny tried to heed the warning bells that seemed to be going off in the dank recesses of her mind.

Don't get involved with someone outside of your social sphere. Don't let physical attraction sway you. Don't let the fact that his skin is so soft and his body so hard and his smile so seductive turn your head. Be strong. You have a plan. Don't let mere emotions get in the way of a psychologically sound plan.

She blinked.

Colt grinned.

She was breathing his breath. And he, hers. Her heart pounded. She pulled her lower lip between her teeth. His gaze followed the movement.

Over at the other end of the pool, her sisters were mounting the shoulders of her cousins. The air was suddenly filled with shouts and their mesmerizing eye contact was broken.

Thank heavens.

"Chicken!" Georgia shouted. "Chicken time!"

"Come on, you guys! Let's play chicken!" Carolina ordered, organizing a pool game and insisting that Colt and Ginny play, too.

Before she knew what hit her, Ginny felt herself lifted to Colt's broad shoulders, and the boys got into strategic positions that would allow the girls to attempt to shove each other into the pool. Okay, perhaps this wasn't such a good idea after all, Ginny thought as she felt Colt cup her calves in his hands. In order to stay upright, she had to press his head into her stomach and fill her fingers with his silky soft hair. Criminy, everything was so dang sensual.

The warm temperature of the water, the warmer temperature of her cheeks, the sultry summer breezes, the tiki torches flickering, the stars twinkling, the romantic hula music piped in from the overhead speakers, the way his muscles rippled beneath her thighs.

It was practically impossible to turn herself off to this barrage of physical and emotional stimulus. Thankfully, she was a professional and could recognize this problem as simply misplaced attachment.

Yes. That was it. No doubt stemming from the disorientation at being away from the conditioned behaviors of her comfort zone.

Having put this demon to bed, she felt a bit better about tangling her body around Colt's in such a hedonistic fashion. Choosing to ignore her jumbled emotions, she tossed off her wayward thoughts and concentrated on pulverizing her sisters.

Over and over, she pushed them—screaming and laughing, of course—into the pool. She was still as competitive as ever, she was pleased to note. Ginny could sense Colt's admiration in the way he'd slap her hand with every point they'd make, and hold on to her fingertips for just a tad longer than necessary.

Finally tired of being humiliated, Carolina announced, "Hey, you guys, I'm starving. How 'bout we rustle up a couple of pizzas?"

"Sounds good!" Hank said.

Georgia and Kenny nodded.

"I could eat a whole one myself," Kenny admitted.

"Great. I'll call that delivery place in Hidden Valley, and after we change our clothes we'll all meet in Ginny's room. You know where it is."

Still seated upon Colt's shoulders, Ginny's jaw

dropped. "*My* room? Wait a minute! I need to go to bed. I've been up since—"

Carolina groaned. "Ginny, would you just relax for once in your life?"

Relax? Ginny scowled. Isn't that what she'd planned to do all day long? Curl up in her jammies with a movie and snooze in front of the TV? Alone? She'd been down here far longer than she'd intended, horsing around.

Georgia ignored her sister's sour expression. "Ginny, the guys know where your room is. All our stuff is already there, and plus, you have the biggest entertainment center." Georgia peered down into Hank's face. "She has the latest surround-sound home-theater system, a collection of rockin' DVDs and enough beanbag chairs so that we can all spread out."

Hank nodded. "Patsy's old room," he said, referring to his older, married sister.

"Besides," Carolina called over her shoulder as she got out of the pool, "her room is already a mess, so no worries. Right, Gin-gin?"

Ginny simply stared at them, marveling at their audacity.

"Okay, then, Ginny's room it is."

Since Big Daddy's sons all took turns working the ranch, the three men lived a mile or so down the road in the bunkhouses that Big Daddy provided for the ranch hands. They all piled into Colt's Durango and headed home to change. Eager for pizza and movies, not to mention the vivacious company of their spirited cousins, they sped down the dusty road, beyond the barns and stables.

"They've sure grown up," Hank noted from the back

seat as he poked his head between his brother and Colt. "Too bad they're our cousins."

Kenny snorted. "And what would you do with them if they weren't, college boy?"

Though he didn't answer, Hank's grin said it all.

The cab filled with easy laughter.

"You and Ginny seemed to pick up right about where you left off." Kenny eyeballed Colt at this observation.

Keeping his gaze on the road, Colt cleared his throat and shrugged, still a little dazed over the day's turn of events. "Uh, yeah."

"She's a real cutie."

"I'll say," Hank chimed in.

"Mmm." Colt nodded.

Kenny shifted his gaze back to Hank. "Kinda uptight, though."

Colt frowned. "I don't get that from her."

"No?" Kenny and Hank exchanged a quick grin.

"No."

Colt frowned. They didn't understand Ginny at all, if they mistook her maturity for tension. But then, they were young. Didn't appreciate the nuances of a real woman yet.

Colt guided the Durango into the gully where surrounding a good-size fishing pond lay their individual cabins. They wasted no time parking and rushing to their own places to get cleaned up.

These days, Colt bunked with Kenny in a two-bedroom cabin, and Hank shared the bunkhouse next door with three college interns who were there that summer to learn some large-animal vet skills. When the three interns weren't working their tails off, they were studying for exams and writing papers. Hank said it was like living with phantoms. Phantoms that snored.

Colt peeled off his damp clothing and tossed it in the hamper. Then he stood in front of his closet and wondered what to wear, which was unusual, considering he normally didn't care about stuff like that. But tonight was different.

Ginny was here.

Ginny. Virginia Brubaker, childhood friend and one completely hot mama. Good grief, when had she gone and gotten so…sexy? He'd been afraid the pool was going to begin boiling when he'd pulled her into his lap. And kissing her? Oh, baby.

What had started out as a silly prank instigated by her goofy sisters had seriously scarred his brain. For life. He'd never be able to kiss another woman without comparing the softness of the lips, the fit of the mouth, the taste of the sweet breath with…

Ginny.

Kissing her was like kissing a thundercloud. Colt sighed as he pulled on a clean T-shirt. It had definitely been an encounter of the third, fourth and fifth kind….

Yessiree-bob, Ginny had grown into a looker. Gobs of auburn hair, all soft and sort of curly, and blue-gray eyes that snapped with life. In spite of the new and improved body, she still had all the things he'd loved about her as a young girl: brains, sense of humor, spirit of adventure, a generous soul and a typically Brubaker love of family and its traditions.

Being an only child, family ties carried an incredible lure for Colt. When they were kids, he always wanted to be near Ginny because of her huge, noisy, chaotic family. That, and the fact that she had such empathy and concern and caring for all creatures. He loved her then, though he would never have admitted it. Besides, his father was always warning him not to get too emotionally involved with the Brubaker girls.

Memories of a feisty, freckled ten-year-old tugged at the corners of his lips. Man, she'd been bossy. She'd organized every game they ever played. And no matter how hard she played, she always managed to look cool and serene and put together. He'd lived to mess her up.

It was wonderful just to be in her company. He hadn't realized, till he'd absconded with her to the pool, how much he'd missed her. Instantly, he was a boy again. Happy. Carefree. And connected. His ally was back.

Hard to believe this evening was the first time he'd laid eyes on her in nearly eight years. With the exception of news that filtered through Miss Clarise and his mother, well, he'd pretty much lost contact because of the natural course of his own destiny.

He'd earned a master's degree, worked his way into a management position here at the Circle BO and then…

Then there'd been his engagement to Renee.

Colt wondered at the sudden tightness in his jaw at the mere flicker of Renee's memory. He'd spent an inordinate amount of time trying not to think about that woman. Ginny would surely have a field day with that. Probably have him reclining on her couch a couple times a week. Although, come to think of it, any time spent on Ginny's couch sounded pretty good.

His grin faded as he thought about dredging up his relationship with Renee for Ginny's scrutiny. Their breakup had been as much his fault as Renee's, which is why he probably put a cork in the anger. Wasn't sure where to direct it.

Good old Renee.

Pretty. Smart. Sassy.

Social climber.

She'd been only too happy to date Colt as a way to get onto the Circle BO property and mix it up with the socially elite. However, the very second that the playboy-next-door paid her a bit of attention, Renee was gone.

She was married to an oilman now. Drove a fancy car, lived in a fancy house, wore fancy clothes and watched her husband philander with a pretty fancy assortment of other women.

He sighed. Curious mix, this empathy and resentment. For now, keeping his feelings bottled up made perfect sense. Renee was getting what she deserved. And he? Well, he had a party waiting up at the big house. Stopping to rationalize his excitement over a simple pizza and movie wasn't part of this evening's plan. He'd spent far too much time in a social wasteland of his own making over the past two years.

Time to have a little fun.

He didn't run in Ginny's circle and never would. She was born to power and privilege and wealth. Colt was born to work for her family. Ah, well. No matter. Tonight was strictly for jollies.

Tomorrow, he'd slip back into the wasteland.

Chapter Three

The large pizza boxes on Ginny's coffee table now sported nothing but crumbs. Sated by pepperoni and Canadian bacon and pineapple, the crowd lounged in Ginny's parlor and watched a popular thriller on her big screen. The four cousins were sprawled out in the four huge beanbag chairs, while Ginny and Colt reclined on the couch, feet propped on the coffee table. The lights were out, save the flicker from the TV.

Down in front, Kenny and Hank mimicked the hero's macho dialogue and made such hysterically dry remarks about the plot that Carolina and Georgia were crying and clutching their middles with laughter. The hilarity was enough to bring down the rafters at certain points but, for once, Ginny didn't notice, so focused was she on Colt's low voice.

"—why I'm not surprised you ended up in psychology." Colt angled his head against the cushions and regarded her thoughtfully. "I should have figured as much. You always were trying to analyze us back when we were kids."

"That's because you were crazy." She turned on her side to face him, a rueful grin playing at her lips. "And I can see you still are."

Colt chuckled. "Where are you living now?"

"I have an apartment outside Dallas. But I still have a lot of stuff stored back in California at school that I'll have to deal with as soon as I find a permanent home."

"You gonna stay in Dallas?"

"I don't know. Right now I have work there and my family is all here, so…I guess I'll just have to see where life takes me." She shrugged. "So. You were an Aggie. With a master's degree, no less."

"Yeah. You never did tell me how you knew all that."

"I have my ways."

"My mother, no doubt."

"And Miss Clarise. Very newsy Christmas cards. They're proud of their boy."

Colt grinned.

"Are you planning on following in your father's footsteps and staying on here at the Circle BO?"

"For now."

Ginny went very still at the two small words. Hank and Kenny were acting out a ridiculous fight scene, thrashing about on the floor. Boisterously, Carolina and Georgia encouraged their nonsense.

"Aren't you going to stay here until you retire, like your dad?" Ginny couldn't begin to explain the feelings of disappointment caused by the idea that Colt might not be here forever. She'd always taken it for granted that everything at the Circle BO would remain constant. Stable. Secure. Ridiculous, she knew, but still...

Colt hunched his shoulders. "I don't plan on being here much past next year. Not that I don't love working for your uncle, and it's great to be following in my dad's footsteps and all, but I have my own life to live. My own plans."

Ginny lay against the back of the couch. *He did?* A sudden stab of jealousy seared her gut. Was he involved with someone? Thinking about marriage? Settling down? Children? When she realized her jaw was sagging most unattractively, she snapped her mouth closed. Why was she obsessing this way? Until she'd arrived that afternoon, Colt and his future hadn't really entered her mind.

She was overly tired. *That, and that blasted kiss.* It had done something to short-circuit her brain. As calmly as possible, Ginny asked, "Where will you go?" She could sense Colt's excitement as he began to outline his plans.

"Right now I'm in the process of buying a parcel of land about fifty miles south of here."

"*Fifty* miles?" She brandished a faux smile. Sounded like a million miles. If he wasn't going to live at the Circle BO anymore, she'd have no excuse to run into him. To rekindle the joys of a youth that she was only beginning to realize she missed. Colt seemed to be the only person that could bring all that stuff out in her.

"Mmm, hmm. I'm going to run a dude ranch. You've seen the movie *City Slickers*?"

Dully, Ginny nodded.

"It'll be kind of like that. Tenderfeet from all over will come to learn ranch life. Riding horses, herding cattle, learning to rope a steer, brand it, you know, the big-animal stuff and, after they pass muster, barbecuing and square dance lessons. I just figure if I have to work for a living, I might as well be doing something I enjoy."

Ginny had to admit, it did sound like a boatload of fun. By comparison, her future seemed positively tame. Cultured. Citified. Everything she'd worked so hard to be suddenly loomed…drearily ahead. She and Brandon—or whoever—would nurture their staid careers while Colt was out hootin' and hollerin' it up with a bunch of city folks who were trying to find themselves.

Just like she'd be in a few years.

While the light of the TV flashed across his dreamy expression, Ginny burrowed into the squishy leather of the couch and listened to Colt fantasize, just as she had when they were little. She hadn't felt this invigorated and warm and secure and relaxed and…and…*confused* for years.

As the evening wore on, Carolina made a pitcher of lemonade and microwaved bags of popcorn at the wet bar. The *pop, pop, pop* and its accompanying aroma filled the air. Soon, bowls were passed out with one for Colt and Ginny to share. Occasionally, their hands would bump as they munched and talked, and sipped and laughed, and simply reveled in the childlike joys of reliving their youth.

While Colt laid out his vision for Ginny, her gaze drank in the changes of the last eight years. Without censorship, she allowed her thoughts to wander into forbidden territory. It was well and truly amazing. Colt had gone from being a whip-thin young man to a full-grown man. For some dumb reason, she hadn't expected that. She rested a fluffy piece of popcorn against her lower lip and stared.

Psychologically speaking, he'd turned out very well. The utterly manly self-confidence. The roguish lift to his eyebrow. The sexy curl to his upper lip. The unruly shock of coffee-colored hair falling over his eye that he was constantly pushing out of his face. Okay, there was nothing psychological about his hair, but it was different now. Awkwardly, she searched for a safe place to rest her gaze, studiously avoiding the granite thighs, the steely arms, the broad, powerful chest and the narrow hips and focusing instead on his earlobe.

That seemed safe enough.

Until a vision of herself nibbling there had her stomach all aflutter. Ginny squirmed as his mellifluous baritone rumbled forth. She could only attribute this insanity to her sisters' bad influence.

Oh well. Never mind. She was on vacation. Perhaps, just this once, she could forgive herself a little whimsy.

So, it was with unusual candor that she heard herself ask, "Are you taken?"

Colt didn't seem to think her abrupt change of subject all that odd. "No. I was. Once. But that's over."

"What happened?"

Hand to jaw, he slowly scratched at the five o'clock shadow gone midnight. "We…she…" He shrugged. "I guess you could say she, Renee, was looking for someone from a particular background and I wasn't it. She was looking for an upwardly mobile lifestyle and I was looking for love."

Ginny stared at him as myriad thoughts raced through her brain. Poor Colt. Dumb Renee. Then again, wasn't what Renee had done exactly what she was planning to do?

No.

It wouldn't be like that. Surely his fiancée hadn't taken the psychological ramifications of her choices into consideration. If she had, clearly they'd still be together. What she had planned with Brandon was far different from Renee's gold-digging scheme.

Somewhat mollified by that rationalization, Ginny allowed her gaze to caress Colt's profile.

Poor Colt. Stupid, stupid Renee. Why, he would have been a real catch for her.

Like Brandon is for me, she reminded herself and leaned back a bit when she realized she could feel Colt's warm breath tickling the stray hairs of her ponytail.

"What about you?" Colt asked. "You taken?"

"Me?" Feeling awkward, she emitted some strangled laughter. "No. Not me. Not yet. No time. Plus, I have a kind of a…a…a sort of a plan, you know, for that."

Eyebrows raised, he asked, "A plan?"

"Well, yeah. I've always believed that if you're ever going to get anything done, you kind of have to have a plan." She hoped to redirect his thoughts. "Kind of like you and your dude ranch plans. Those are wonderful plans. Tell me more."

The diversionary tactic did not work.

"No. Enough about me. I bore me. Tell me about these marriage plans of yours."

"Oh, now, come on, you don't bore me. Really!"

"Ginny."

She could tell by the tone of his voice that he wasn't going to give up anytime soon. "Oh well, all right. When I was in college, I focused my dissertation on *The Influence of Perceived Physical Attractiveness Versus the Effects of Environment upon Selection of Love Objects.*"

"Come again?"

Ginny laughed. "To put it in layman's terms, I re-searched what makes a happy marriage."

"Thank you."

The air-conditioning was causing gooseflesh to rise, so Ginny reached behind her, grabbed a throw and arranged it over her lap as she spoke. Colt took one end and pulled the blanket across his own legs.

"Anyway, in my career, I've seen so much heart-break." She sighed heavily and looked into his eyes. "For example, I counseled one couple—Mr. and Mrs.... er...let's call them the Smiths. Anyway, they grew up on opposite sides of the tracks in families of vastly different backgrounds. He was rich. She was poor. He was an athlete, she was scholarly. He was bold, she was timid. Get the theme?"

Colt nodded, giving her his undivided attention, in spite of the exuberance coming from the party on the floor.

"Anyway, they ran into each other at a wedding after they'd grown up, and it was love at first sight. They married in haste and repented at leisure. Their problem?"

Colt lifted his hands. "Uh, she was a nag?"

"No, you goof. They were complete *opposites*. Going on the old 'opposites attract' theory. And just look where it landed them."

"Where?"

"In therapy!"

"So?"

"So, I'm not going to let that happen to me. I know it may sound kind of callous, but I'm going to approach my marriage with common sense. Not let the heart do the leading."

"But what about love?" Colt squinted at her with

that funny look she got from just about everyone she explained her theories to.

Ginny plucked at the fringe on their blanket. "Love is one of those things that I believe will grow out of mutual desires, goals, mind-set and lifestyle. Not out of passion."

"Just so I'm on the same page here—" Colt's eyebrows locked "—you are interested in finding someone of a certain…social background?"

"Yes. But not like Renee."

"Hello? Exactly like Renee."

"No. She didn't know what she was doing."

Colt hooted at that.

"What?" Miffed, Ginny gave his shoulder a little shove. "She's nothing like me."

"Nothing." Compressed air hissed from between his smirking lips. "Nothing at all, I guess, seeing as how you're gonna be up-front about it."

"Of course. I believe in being completely forthright. Saying what I want."

"Saying what you want."

"Yes. No use beating around the bush."

"I guess not."

A pall had descended over their cozy chat. Ginny sensed that Colt was disapproving and though this made her sad and more than a little uncomfortable, she forced herself not to let his opinion get her down.

After all, she knew her methods were controversial. But they were also right. Time would prove her methods sound. Of this, Ginny was sure.

For over two hours now they'd been completely absorbed by their conversation, enveloped in their little cocoon under the blanket on the couch. Shoulder to shoulder they sat, arguing about her plan in whispered voices and so involved that when the lights popped back on and Kenny turned off the TV, they blinked at their surroundings in surprise.

"Great movie, huh, guys?" Hank asked them, sarcasm dripping.

It had escaped no one that Colt and she hadn't paid a bit of attention to anyone but each other.

"Uh, yeah," Colt said, grinning. "Loved it."

"Uh-huh. Me too." Ginny stared at the floor.

Following a brief discussion of the plot and some wide, groan-filled yawns, everyone slowly dragged themselves to their feet and headed for the door. After a round of big sloppy hugs good-night, it was Ginny's turn to embrace Colt. And though she was peeved with him, she was surprised to note that old zing once again. Good grief, she thought as she set him away from her. What was with this stupid zing?

She should stay away from these guys. Their juvenile style was lending hers to flights of fancy.

"Hey, Ginny and Colt." Carolina paused at the door. "We've decided to go on a picnic tomorrow after church. The pond in the north section has a rope swing. Kenny and Hank will bring the paddleboats in the ATV trailer. We'll pack a basket of sandwiches and fruit, pop and beer. You coming?"

"Uh…" Caught completely off guard, Ginny and Colt exchanged befuddled looks.

Colt shrugged. "What the heck? Sure. It's Sunday, it's not like we have anything better to do. Right?"

So much for her plans to stay away from these guys. "Right."

"Great. It's a date." Carolina turned to follow her sister and cousins into the hall. "See y'all tomorrow."

"G'night," Ginny called.

"G'night," Colt returned.

She watched him move out and down the hall after her sisters and cousins and gently closed the door. Leaning against the smooth mahogany surface, she gave her head a little shake.

It was so disconcerting to be around someone who knew her so well and was not afraid to voice his opinions. She expected this much from her sisters, as they were always ribbing her, but Colt? Somehow, when he chastised her, it carried a bit of a sting.

No matter.

She was the psychologist here. Not him.

A light knock at her door startled Ginny as she swept the last of the pizza crumbs into the wastebasket. She dusted off her hands and checked her appearance in the mirror on her way to the door. Could it be Colt? Had he forgotten something? Perhaps he wanted to continue their conversation?

Carolina, not Colt, was standing in the hall, a hopeful look on her face.

"Sorry to bug you, but I forgot my night cream and my makeup remover." She held up her toothbrush. "And, uh, my toothpaste."

"Did you pack in your sleep?" Ginny groused and, taking a step back, motioned her sister into her room.

Carolina shrugged. "I was in a hurry."

"Try making a list next time."

"Yeah. Right. A list." Carolina headed to the bathroom sink and began to rummage through Ginny's toiletries. "Sho," she burbled around a frothy mouthful of toothpaste, "at Coat's prebby coot, huh?"

"What?" Ginny frowned as she slipped out of her shoes and parallel parked them between two pairs of like style and color.

Carolina noisily spit. "Colt. Cute."

"Uh, yeah. I guess."

"You guess." Carolina snorted and beat her toothbrush on the edge of the sink, then popped it into her sister's toothbrush holder.

Ginny exhaled with a groan. Clearly, Carolina intended to partake in her evening rituals here every night. "Okay, so he's handsome. Lots of men are handsome. It's what's inside that counts."

Carolina hiked her foot up onto the counter and proceeded to slather her leg with Ginny's lotion. "Don't you think Colt is a good man?"

Not wanting to delve too deeply into her various admirations of Colt, Ginny said, "Sure. He's a wonderful man."

"And he deserves a wonderful woman."

"I guess."

"And so…?"

Pressing her fingertips to her throbbing forehead, Ginny gave it a vicious rub. Here it was, midnight, and her sister was in here playing slumber party games. "And so, if you are trying to tell me that you have a thing for Colt, then…" She jerked a blasé little shrug. "Then go for it." Even as Ginny said the words, she knew she didn't mean them.

"Maybe I should," Carolina mused.

This comment irked Ginny, but she wasn't sure why. After all, Carolina could date whomever she wished. Ginny shook off her ire and concentrated on getting dressed for bed. Oh, she was tired. Unfortunately, Carolina was still in the bathroom, pawing through her makeup bag and purse.

"Where's your floss?" Carolina demanded, and then grew still. She held up a business card. "What's this?"

Ginny poked her head out of her nightie and squinted. "Oh. That's just Brandon's business card. Miss Clarise gave it to me after lunch."

A small smile stole over Carolina's lips. "Let's call him."

"Now?" Ginny smirked at the clock. "You're nuts."

"You'd know." Carolina picked up the phone. "C'mon. I dare ya."

"No way. It's midnight. He'll shoot us."

"No he won't. I think he'll be glad you called."

"Carolina..." Ginny affected her most menacing tone. "Put that phone down this instant."

Giggles in her throat, Carolina dialed.

At first, Ginny couldn't believe Carolina had actually done it. Surely her sister was putting her on. "Carolina, knock it off and go to bed."

"Hello." Carolina backed away from Ginny as she approached. "Brandon? Hi! This is Carolina Brubaker. Is it too late to call? You were? Great!"

"Oh, sure." Ginny's tone was snide. "Carolina, enough of your little pranks. Go to bed."

Carolina laughed with delight. "Yes, that's Ginny. Uh-huh. Actually, she's the reason I'm calling."

Ginny rolled her eyes and loaded her own tooth-brush, and began to give her teeth a vicious brushing. Funny. Very funny.

"She was feeling a little shy but wanted to call and let you know we were all here for the summer, and per-haps to invite you over for lunch soon. Yes. Uh-huh."

Carolina laughed. "Right. She's always been the social organizer. You remember that."

"Shtop it," Ginny grunted as she brushed. "You not funny."

"Anyway, here she is." Carolina handed the phone to Ginny.

When she heard Brandon's smooth voice coming from the earpiece, Ginny froze. "Uhllo?"

"Ginny?" This time she was really gonna kill Carolina. Just as soon as she caught her. For Carolina was already skipping down the hallway, hooting with laughter.

"An ooo hold, pleash?"

"Uh, sure."

Ginny spit, rinsed and then stared at the phone. Good heavens. Brandon was on the line and she hadn't prepared a thing to say. Slowly, she raised the instrument to her head and cleared her throat. "Hello, Brandon," she said, affecting her most cultured tone. "I'm so very sorry about bothering you at this later hour. Clearly, my sister did not note the time before she dialed."

"Hey, that's cool. So, you guys are in Hidden Valley for the summer?"

"Uh, yes." Phew. At least he wasn't yelling. As Brandon chatted, Ginny groped for something witty to say. But what? She wiped her clammy palm on a hand towel. Good grief, she hadn't seen him since Christmas, a year and a half ago. Although, he *had* exhibited more than a passing interest back then. And he'd even written the occasional letter to her while she was away at college, encouraging her to look him up as soon as she got to the Circle BO. She just hadn't planned on looking him up quite this soon.

Much to her dismay, her door swung open and Carolina burst in, dragging a grinning Georgia behind her. They flopped onto her bed and made themselves comfy. Ginny marched to the door, yanked it open and gestured for them to leave, but they only exchanged amused glances.

"Uh-huh. Oh. Uh-huh. Is that right?" Gracious, she'd lost the thread of this conversation and had no idea what Brandon was prattling on about. "Well, it's been just wonderful talking with you. I should probably let you go. You must be tired."

"No," Brandon said, but his yawn spoke volumes.

Mortified, Ginny shot a murderous glance at Carolina. Clearly, they'd woken him. As he dredged up more polite conversation, her sisters sat there and made goo-goo eyes, and aped about in the background. She snapped her fingers at them, to shut them up, but they only snapped back.

Ginny had to plug her ear and shut her eyes in an attempt to ignore them. "Brandon, I understand that you and your family will be joining us tomorrow night for a barbecue."

Yes, it seemed Brandon had been looking forward to it all week.

After what seemed like endless stilted conversation, Ginny was finally able to gracefully lead them to their goodbyes. "Okay then. I look forward to tomorrow."

"So do I."

"Great. Okay then."

"Okay then," Carolina said to Georgia.

"Okay then," Georgia replied.

Ginny clapped her hand over the mouthpiece. *"Shut up,"* she mouthed. "Well," she chirped at Brandon. "Okay then."

What the devil else could she say? That was her third *Okay then,* but for the love of Mike, all other rational conversation eluded her. She did not have the history with Brandon that she had with Colt, so of course, conversation was nowhere near as easy.

"Okay then, bye now." She felt like a complete idiot.

"Okay. Bye." Brandon yawned and blessedly, they rang off.

"You brats!" She threw the phone and it glanced off Carolina's foot. "Get out. Find your own rooms."

"Is this the gratitude we get for setting you up with your honey?"

"I'm perfectly able to take care of my own love life. Go away. Now."

"Awww," Georgia grumbled.

"But we love to hang around you!" Carolina thrust out her lower lip. "We are good for you! You need us to help you loosen up and enjoy life before you wake up one day and realize that all the fun has passed you by." On their way out the door, they draped their arms around Ginny's neck and noisily kissed her cheeks.

And Ginny, as always, found it impossible to stay mad at them.

Chapter Four

The next morning, right after church, Colt, Kenny and Hank called for the girls up at the big house. Laughing and joking as only old friends and family can, they all piled into three, four-wheeled all-terrain vehicles and headed to the pond for their picnic. Kenny and Carolina rode together, towing several paddleboats on a trailer. Hank and Georgia hauled the fishing poles and gear, and Colt and Ginny packed all the lunch fixings, a huge picnic hamper, beach blankets, sunscreen, beach towels and just about everything they might need for a lazy day of fun.

As they crested a knoll above the picnic area and paused in the road, Ginny's breath caught in her throat and involuntarily she tightened her grip around Colt's middle.

She'd forgotten how beautiful this place was.

Down in a tree-filled gully sat a giant pond, its surface so glassy blue that the catfish could be seen jumping for bugs. In the middle of the pond was a floating dock. A wooded area surrounded over three-quarters of the water, keeping it reasonably shady and cool for the better part of the day. A shady pergola, covered with climbing vines, was perched at the edge of the woods. A picnic table and barbecue pit were situated underneath.

So many wonderful summer picnics. Where had the time gone?

Glancing over his shoulder, Colt grinned at her, seeming to sense the buoyancy in her mood at being home again.

Once they reached the pergola—since the mercury was already pushing eighty in the shade—they all agreed to dash down to the pond and splash around before they unpacked a thing. As they had when they were kids, they indulged in a manner of water horseplay and when they'd had their fill, they all gathered around the picnic table half-starved and gobbled a sumptuous repast. After their bellies were sated, they spread out blankets in a sunny patch on the beach.

Much to Ginny's chagrin, the rousing conversation turned to her "plans" for her love life. It was with great interest that everyone forced her into outlining her goals. They all laughed and teased her without mercy, with the lone exception of Colt, who lay back and watched her through the slits of his eyes.

So. She was serious about this manhunt. He swallowed the disappointment that crowded his throat, determined to withhold final judgment until he'd heard her out.

"You know," Ginny huffed, "I thought this subject might come up, so I brought some materials—" she squinted at her sisters with murderous eyes "——to test you."

"A test?" Kenny's and Hank's noses wrinkled in complaint. Especially Hank who'd just finished his first year of college.

"Yes. One of several tests designed to decipher your particular personality type, and to let you know what type would best suit you as a mate."

The boys groaned.

"I don't need a test to tell you the type that suits me." Kenny's eyebrows bobbed.

Georgia groaned. "Yeah, I'm sure any one of the *Baywatch* lifeguards would suit you."

"I want to have Yasmine Bleeth's children."

"Yeah, well, get in line."

"Guys. Relax. This will be fun," Ginny insisted, ignoring their banter as she smoothly extracted testing materials from her bag.

Though he was feeling the skeptic, Colt couldn't suppress a grin. Still as organized as ever. He liked that about Ginny. Oddly enough, it made him feel somehow secure. As if she would be able to save the day with a simple pen and pad of paper. Ginny Brubaker was smart, savvy and confident. Didn't spend her days clowning around like some people, but instead made goals.

And hey, he may not admire all her idiotic plans, but at least she was in there swinging. Not waiting around for life to come to her. No. Ginny was a player. Out on the field. Come what may, she'd have a lot to talk about in life's locker room.

Colt propped himself up on his elbows and lowered his sunglasses to see better.

"Okay. First of all, just for fun, I'm going to administer a simple inkblot test. This is an older test that is probably the best-known projective technique."

She didn't seem to notice the puzzled looks exchanged by the gang.

"It was developed by a man named Hermann Rorschach, a Swiss psychiatrist—"

"Yeah, yeah—" Georgia feigned a snore "—get to the fun part."

"Okay. I have here ten inkblots. I'll show them to you one by one and ask you what you see, in a free-association manner. I'll be evaluating your responses, using three different categories. Detail, determinants and content."

"Okay already, just do it." Carolina was getting impatient.

"Who wants to go first?"

"I guess I'm man enough to step up to the plate," Kenny blustered.

Everyone groaned.

"Kenny..." Ginny held up card number one. "What do you see?"

Kenny frowned. "Two poodles dancing."

Hank guffawed at that.

"Carolina?"

"Uh...hmm. I see a supermodel's pelvis."

"Ohhh? Where?" Hank demanded.

"See the bones sticking out? Right there." Carolina pointed.

"Ahhh, yeah."

Ginny ignored them. "Georgia?"

"A bleeding bat."

"A bleeding...*bat?*"

"Yeah. What's that mean?"

"It means we need to delve a whole lot deeper. When we get home, you're on the couch."

"Oh, great."

Everyone laughed. "Hank?"

"Well, now that you mention it, I see a bleeding bat, too."

Ginny rolled her eyes. "Okay, you two are perfect for each other." Again, the laughter rumbled.

"Colt, what do you see?"

"I see a beautiful woman holding a card."

"You do?" At first, Ginny studied the blot, until she realized that Colt was referring to her.

He found her blush endearing.

She proceeded to quiz them on the other nine cards and, frowning in deep concentration, administered several other tests as well, even as the laughter rose and fell around her. Colt propped his chin on his wrists and marveled. She was the consummate professional.

"I'll compile your answers and let you know your results later this week," she promised.

"Are you going to test Brandon?" Georgia wanted to know.

Ginny lifted a casual shoulder. "I thought I might."

"Brandon?" The little hairs on the back of Colt's neck suddenly stood at attention as he rolled on his side to face Ginny.

"Brandon McGraw," Carolina told him. "The number one lab rat in Ginny's plan."

"He's not a lab rat." Irritated, Ginny slapped the inkblots, which lay in her lap. "I simply feel that he may have the criteria I'm looking for in a future mate."

"Criteria. Love that." Carolina flopped back on her towel.

Ginny disregarded her dramatics. "You know Brandon, Colt? He lives with his family just down the road apiece. They're oilmen, too."

Colt nodded. An oilman. Like the guy Renee married.

"I met him at a Christmas party Big Daddy threw last year in Dallas. We've e-mailed from time to time, and he's been very encouraging. He's coming to the party tonight."

He could feel the muscles in his jaw twitching. "Why Brandon McGraw?"

Everyone's eyes swung from Colt to Ginny.

"Oh, for many reasons," Ginny patiently explained. "We grew up together, we come from similar backgrounds, we are about the same age, oh, there are a million reasons that we might be compatible. And...I guess...back when I was going over possibilities and reviewing options in my acquaintance, he just seemed like the obvious place to start. I won't know for sure, of course, until I run him through a few tests."

Everyone—save Colt—groaned and gagged and, hands to throats, rolled around on their towels.

"Knock it off," Ginny groused. "You are all acting like children. Except for Colt. He seems to be the only adult among you."

No, Colt wanted to shout. He'd be pretending to gag, too, but the bile that rose in his throat made the prospect of retching all too real. He lay there, surprised by the irritation he felt welling up inside. As the others gave Ginny hell for her wacky plan, Colt began to realize that he was growing...*jealous?*

That was weird.

He and Ginny were merely old family friends. Plus, he knew in his head that all of this was really none of his business.

He forced himself to loosen up. To relax. To take deep, calming breaths. Chill out, buddy. So she wanted to test Brandon McGraw. It was none of his affair.

Besides, certainly her tests would prove that Brandon was not the man for her. They were far too alike. Ginny would never stand for being controlled by a guy like Brandon. Colt didn't know Brandon that well, but from what he could tell, the guy was the type to want a bubbleheaded socialite on his arm. Not some intense, overly analytical shrink with legs that went on for absolutely ever....

Brandon and Ginny were not a match.

Nope.

Somewhat mollified by this rationalization, Colt's spirits lifted and he allowed himself to join in on the teasing.

"Y'all just shut up." Leading with her chin, Ginny stood—and polka-dotted bottom swaying—marched to the water's edge. "Last one to the dock is a bleeding bat."

Pandemonium ensued as, pushing and shoving, everyone raced for the dock.

As the sun arced across the sky, Kenny and Hank snoozed out on the dock, fishing poles in their hands, bobbers bobbing. Carolina lounged on the shore and read fashion magazines, while Georgia reclined in the pergola and painted her toenails.

Ginny and Colt paddled lazily around the lakelike pond in one of the boats they'd brought.

Ginny gave her watch a languid glance. Nearly three. "We should all probably think about leaving in an hour or so, so that there will be time to pack up all this stuff, and get back and dress for the party tonight."

"Mmm." Colt nodded, not feeling inclined to attend a party where Ginny would be wooing the boy next door. Though he'd told himself over and over again to drop it, thoughts of Ginny and the oh-so-wrong-for-her Brandon continued to plague him. "Ginny?"

"Hmm?" Her head lolled in his direction.

"You really believe that you couldn't make a life with a man who wasn't born with a silver spoon in his mouth?"

"I think that the fact that I come from money would cause problems."

"What problems?"

"Ego, for one."

"A regular guy couldn't handle the fact that you come from money?"

"Yes."

"And what if your family loses everything. What then?"

"Not likely."

"Play along."

"Colt, it's not the money. It's the lifestyle."

"So, sharing the same background is the only way to ensure compatibility."

"To my way of thinking, yes."

"Why didn't you play with Brandon when we were growing up? He was always around."

"I don't know." Ginny chuckled. "I had you."

"My point exactly. You weren't interested in a future oilman. You wanted to play with the blue-collar kid."

"Yeah, but Colt, you and I, we weren't *married*. We were playmates."

"You make marriage sound about as enticing as a case of rickets."

"I do?"

"Mmm, hmm. And I have to wonder why. Your parents are blissful. And they married for love. In fact, everyone in your family has, and so far, so good."

Ginny grinned. "Luck?"

Reaching into the water, Colt splashed Ginny, causing her to squeal. "You're hopeless."

She splashed him back. "No, I'm not. I'm right. And you'll see. I begin my seduction of Brandon McGraw tonight. Any hints on how to get him to sit up and take notice?"

Deflated, Colt sighed. She really did see him as just some overgrown playmate if she was asking him how to attract another man. He pulled his baseball cap lower on his forehead so that she couldn't see the emotions that warred. *He* might not be right for Ginny, but *dammit,* neither was Brandon.

"Just be yourself," was his advice. "And be sure to give him some of those really fun tests of yours."

And, please, oh please, whatever you do, don't kiss him. He dragged a palm over his mouth and swallowed a groan. For Colt knew one kiss was all it would take for Brandon to fall.

The old-fashioned Southern barbecue was one of Big Daddy Brubaker's fortes. He was well known for his fantastic parties, and people far and wide traveled to the Circle BO to attend. And though everyone had a rollicking good time, no one had more fun at one of his soirées than Big Daddy himself.

Colt and the guys arrived from their bunkhouses at the same time Ginny and her sisters appeared on the scene, and Big Daddy nearly tackled them all in his effusive greeting.

"Why, lookie here," the elfin man crowed, finally holding the girls at arm's length after peppering their cheeks with kisses. "You gals are pretty enough to make a man plow through a stump. Isn't that right, boys?"

Colt grinned. "Prettier than a pie supper."

Laughter braying, Big Daddy clapped Colt on the back. "My mama, God rest her soul, used to say that all the time. Those were the days. Back when Ginny's daddy and me were so broke we couldn't buy hay for a nightmare. But all us kids were happy just the same. Well, okay. You youngsters have fun now. Go on with ya. I'll be back later to claim a dance or two."

"Okay, Big Daddy," Ginny murmured, and watched her uncle trot off into the crowd.

Because he didn't want to lose her in the swarming masses, Colt took Ginny by the hand and ambled after her sisters and cousins toward the buffet table. At least he told himself this was the reason for tucking her fingers into the crook of his arm. Luckily, Ginny seemed too preoccupied with people watching to notice. Colt had to admit, there was a lot to see.

The rolling lawn was festooned with white tents draped with mosquito netting and filled with linen-covered tables. White Japanese paper lanterns bobbed on strands of wire, and on every tabletop candles glowed from floral centerpieces. Already in full-tilt boogie, a country-western band up onstage had folks on the parquet dance floor jumpin' and jivin' to the beat. Waiters deftly weaved through the throng, delivering hors d'oeuvres and Chef was attending the pig that slowly turned on a spit. The summer breezes mingled the tantalizing scents of food, hickory smoke, freshly mowed grass and roses in bloom.

Colt nodded and smiled at familiar faces as he strolled by with Ginny. Though he knew it was stupid, he couldn't help but indulge in the little fantasy that he was the object of her search for the perfect man. That tonight, he fulfilled her every wish, or list or…or…criteria, or whatever the hell she wanted, and that good old Brandon, who'd just arrived, by the way, would simply drop dead.

But that wasn't gonna happen. And he needed to come to grips with that now. Before he made a big old fool of himself in front of just about everyone he knew.

They arrived at the buffet table just as Big Daddy discovered Brandon and his parents up by the bandstand. Enthusiastic pleasantries were exchanged as the old man pumped Brandon's arm nearly out of its socket. Colt knew the instant that Ginny became aware of Brandon's presence.

She stiffened as their gazes met.

Brandon winked.

Ginny clutched Colt's arm and swallowed, a tremulous smile on her lips. Colt glanced from Ginny to Brandon and back to Ginny. She was still smiling. So was he.

A cold sweat broke out over Colt's body. As a terrible nausea seized his gut, he became hyperaware of the sounds of the laughing crowd, the hissing spit, the depressing lyrics of the country music, and, of course, Big Daddy's booming voice as he welcomed Brandon to his party.

Through her teeth, Ginny hissed, "What now? What do I do now?"

For crying in the night. What the devil did she want from him?

"Go over and talk to him," he chided, growing impatient with her. If she was gonna do this thing, then she should do it and get it the hell over with, and leave him out of it. He could hardly stand the crazy feelings that were swirling in his gut. He wanted to punch Brandon, and the poor guy had done nothing but show up and shake Big Daddy's hand.

Colt was no expert on emotions and the like, but he knew that the deeper he got sucked into this goofy experiment of Ginny's the loonier he'd be. Soon he'd need her services as a doctor.

Taking a deep breath, he nudged her in Brandon's direction, but like a shy little kid, she hung back and hovered behind him.

He pinched the bridge of his nose. "Ginny, he's not going to bite you. Just go up to him and say hello. He's expecting you."

"I know." Still, she did not move.

"What's the problem?"

"I don't know."

"Repressing your desires?" Colt mocked.

"What do you know about repression?"

"It's a defense mechanism that guards against anxiety and guilt by the unconscious exclusion of painful and unacceptable ideas or impulses, such as—" he nodded at Brandon "—deciding to marry the acorn because you like the tree."

Ginny stared at him agog and, blinking, gave her head a little shake. "You learn that in college?"

Colt shrugged. "I had a psych study partner who was always accusing everyone of being repressed." He wouldn't bother to mention that late last night he'd cracked his old psych text to brush up for just such an occasion.

As she laughed, admiration flashed in her eyes and suddenly, Colt felt like a superhero. Able to leap tall Brandons in a single bound.

The country-western band switched to a soulful number as the sun disappeared behind the western hills, bathing the party in shadows. Couples streamed to the dance floor in droves.

"Seems to me you need a little loosening up. Wanna dance? I mean just until Big Daddy turns your fella loose."

It seemed to him that Ginny sighed a huge sigh of relief, even as she bristled. "He's not my *fella*."

Colt smirked. "Yet." Linking his fingers with hers, he led her out to the dance floor, plunging ever deeper into the quagmire of his past, present and rather dubious future with his childhood soul mate.

It felt so right, swaying to the music with her in his arms, her fine, soft hair tickling his chin and jaw. This was the very first time he'd ever held her hip to hip like this. Of course, they hadn't had much call to slow dance when they were kids.

As they moved across the parquet, Colt noticed that Carolina and Georgia had joined Big Daddy and were giggling at something he was saying to Brandon. Unlike Ginny, they were relaxed and clearly having the time of their lives. Carolina was batting her eyes and twirling a blond curl around her forefinger and Georgia was unabashedly singing along with the music.

A grin tugged at the corners of Colt's mouth. Those two were such minxes. Big Daddy was gonna have his hands full with them this summer. Lightly, he pushed at Ginny's cheek with his nose and as he tilted her head back, he could see that she was watching them with a look of yearning in her eyes. Knowing Ginny the way he did, Colt knew she wished she could be having such a relaxed conversation with Brandon.

"Smile."

"Oh." She smiled. "Sorry. I was just thinking."

"Well, stop it."

Again she laughed and clung to him. Again, he was Superman.

Ginny nodded in Brandon and Carolina's direction. "They're having fun."

"Mmm." Protectively, Colt tightened his embrace.

Pulling Ginny's body flush with his, he rubbed his cheek against her temple and ran his hands over her back. She was strong yet delicate. Both physically and emotionally. He sighed and closed his eyes. This was heaven. He didn't care what Ginny said about compatibility

As if Ginny could read his mind, she lifted her head, sliding her cheek alongside his until their noses were a hairbreadth apart, and eyes flashing, looked up at him.

"Hi," he said.

"Hi," she answered, and after a moment, lay her head upon his chest.

"It's good to have you back."

"It's good to be back."

Yep, Colt could stay like this forever.

Unfortunately, all too soon, reality intruded in the form of a tap on the back from Brandon McGraw.

"May I have this dance?'

Colt hesitated. "Uh…Ginny?" *Say no, say no, say no,* he willed.

"Yes," she demurred and awkwardly moved from Colt's embrace to Brandon's. She licked her lips. "How are you, Brandon?"

"Fine, now," he answered with a toothy grin that set Colt on edge. He studied the tall, dark and stereotypically handsome man, hoping to find some flaw in his appearance that would assuage his irritation. But there was none. Brandon McGraw could step onto the set of any movie and play the hero.

Flexing his fists and feeling like yesterday's news, Colt stepped away and left them to become reacquainted and eventually…engaged.

Ginny could scarcely believe it, but she was relieved when Carolina finally approached and tapped her on the shoulder for a dance with Brandon. Not that Brandon was a bad dancer, actually he was rather good. But there was something… Ginny passed it off as the tension that came from trying so hard. Good heavens, keeping up all that stilted conversation really sapped one's energy. She wanted to put her best foot forward with every word, and at the same time evaluate his ideals and values and compare them with her own.

It was exhausting.

As she stepped back and watched Carolina and Brandon high-step it out to the middle of the dance floor, she marveled at the ease with which Carolina and Brandon bantered. That was talent. She felt a stab of envy.

It would really be nice to be so comfortable in one's skin. To be able to toss one's shoes in the middle of the floor and then simply step over them until the next time they were needed. To be able to let go and simply play for the sake of playing.

From the anonymity of the throng, Ginny watched Carolina waltz across the floor with Brandon, head back, mouth open, shoulders bouncing with delicious fun.

Funny how her sister hadn't seen Brandon since Christmas before last, and yet, look at her, all relaxed and chummy. All her life, Ginny could strive for that *joie de vivre* and never achieve even half the merriment that came so naturally to her sisters. Ginny moved into the crowd and swallowed back the feelings of inadequacy.

With a clearing shake, she forced herself to stop focusing on her shortcomings and instead enjoy the moment. So she wasn't a laugh a minute. She had other talents. Talents that someday she was sure would aid her in her relationship with Brandon.

Like a homing pigeon, her feet carried her automatically to Colt's side where she hoped the soothing balm of familiarity would ground her again. He was standing near a group of ranch hands who were busily loading their plates with sloppy barbecue and all the Southern-style trimmings.

"How'd it go?" Colt asked, balancing the neck of his beer bottle against his lower lip before he took a long pull.

Ginny shrugged and picked a cherry tomato from the veggie tray. "Okay, I guess. It'll take time. I shouldn't expect to whip out the Rorschach test on the first day together."

With a laugh, Colt set his empty bottle on a passing tray and extended his hand. "C'mon, let's dance."

"Again?" She glanced over at Brandon. "But what will people think?"

"They'll think that you are dancing and having a good time. Just like they are. Come on."

That was true enough. Brandon was being put through some outlandish two-step routine by Carolina. His grin was positively Cheshire as he stumbled over first her feet then his own.

Fingers twined, Ginny marveled at how easy it was to follow Colt out to the dance floor and step into his embrace. She only wished her turn with Brandon had been as relaxing.

Then again, this wasn't exactly all that relaxing.

There was that doggone *zing* again. That, and the uninvited image of Colt's soft lips moving over her own. Gracious, she had to stop thinking about that. It wasn't healthy. Her breathing came in shallow puffs and she knew she was clinging to Colt a little more tightly than was strictly necessary.

"You okay?" There was concern in his eyes as he bent to peer into her face.

Having his chiseled, curling, completely sexy lips hovering mere inches from her face did nothing to rectify the situation.

"Fine," she chirped. Just…fine.

Or at least she would be, once she…convinced…Brandon to…to…

As the sixty-four-thousand-watt idea illuminated over her head, Ginny paused, stunned.

Of course. That was it.

She needed to convince Brandon to kiss her.

Her eyes narrowed and her jaw firmed with determination. Yes. A romantic moment with Brandon. The sooner the better. She gnawed the inside of her cheek as a case of nerves assaulted her. Tonight even.

Then, and probably only then, would she be able to get Colt's heart-liquefying talents out of her head.

Chapter Five

The rest of the evening passed in a haze of dread and anticipation for Ginny. After midnight, Big Daddy got onstage and made a huge deal out of how excited he was over his three successful nieces. Then he proceeded to embarrass the tar out of Ginny by making her get up on the stage with him and—after touting her talents as a "headshrinker extraordinaire"—cajoled her into singing a karaoke duet version of his all-time favorite song, "Feelings," with him in honor of her profession.

Big Daddy sang like a pawin' bull with his tail up. He mugged for the audience, the fringe on his leather jacket swinging and his ten-gallon hat swimming on his five-gallon head. Ginny found herself giggling more than singing, but Big Daddy didn't seem to notice. Not to be left out, Georgia and Carolina jumped up onstage and, grabbing a befuddled Ginny between them, played the part of her backup singers.

"—feeeeelings of luh-uh-uhvvvv!" the girls shouted, echoing Big Daddy who was now down on his knees, belting out the *woah-woah-woahs* to his flame-faced wife.

Like a summer thunderstorm, a roar of approval rippled through the crowd.

And though Ginny was mortified, there was a part of her that loved the attention. Now and again, she would search out the audience for Brandon's face, but then, like a compass needle to true north, her gaze would swing to Colt. And Colt, unlike the more reserved Brandon, was catcalling and egging her on.

"Yeee-hah, Gin-gin! *Wooooo-hooooooo!* Yeah, baybee! *Swang* that *thang!*"

Big Daddy ended the song by bending each of his nieces back in turn for a noisy kiss on the cheek. The crowd's response rattled the china on the tables.

When it was over, Colt waited at edge of the stage to lift Ginny down and give her a hug. "Ginny girl, you were great! You missed your calling."

"Oh, please." Ginny could swear that even her toes were blushing at his sweet words. Colt always knew just what to say. "Do you think Brandon thought so, too?" Up on tiptoe, she strained to see over the crowd.

"I..." Colt dragged a hand over his jaw and sighed. "Yeah. Sure. I guess so."

She clutched Colt's hand in hers and, giving his arm a little yank, pulled his ear to her mouth.

"Colt, I'm going to ask Brandon if I can walk him to his car in a little while."

No response. No movement, no encouragement, no shrug, no nothing.

"Colt? Did you hear me?"

"I heard ya."

"So, do you think I should do it?"

"You're a big girl. Do what you want."

"Okay, but how?"

"What do you mean, how? Find Brandon. Find his car. Start walking."

"You don't need to be such a grump." Ginny decided to overlook his rusty etiquette, considering the lateness of the hour. Plus, she needed advice on how to handle the next few moments with Brandon. She needed to know how one got this business of the good-night kiss rolling. Being the initiator had never been her strong suit. "So, I was wondering…" She swallowed and stared at the lawn.

"Yeah?"

"I think a small, tasteful kiss would be a good way to declare my intentions to Brandon that I am ready to begin a relationship."

Silence.

"Colt!"

"You think it's time for a kiss."

"You don't think I should do it?"

"What do you care what I think?"

"I don't. I just need some…advice."

Colt's expression grew suspicious. "What kind of advice?"

"Well, how exactly do I get started?"

Colt stared.

"Like, what should I do first?"

"You want me to tell you how to kiss him?"

"No."

"No?"

"I want *him* to kiss *me*."

"Criminy, Ginny, what's the difference?"

"Him kissing me puts me on better psychological footing. Just tell me what to do."

"I can't believe we are having this conversation." Colt gave his temples a vicious rub. "Knowing you, you're not gonna be happy until I give you some pointers."

"No."

After a long, slow shake of his head he said, "Okay, I guess you probably should start out by standing close. Like this." He took an aggressive step toward Ginny, causing her heart to flutter. "Renee used to stand really close. It always worked for me." He shrugged.

"Stand really close. Check."

"Then, I guess your body language should communicate…interest. At the end of the evening, Renee would always lean against my car and look all, you know, uh, provocative."

Even in the gloaming, Ginny could see the pain flash in his eyes. Stupid girl. Shaking off her feelings of anger for Renee, she made mental notes, thumb to fingertips. "Gotcha. Stand close. Use provocative body lingo. Good, good. What else?"

"Well, I guess you should have an expression on your face that's kissable."

"Kissable expression. Check. What kind of expression would that be, exactly?"

"Figure it out. I'm not going to spell out every detail for you."

"Sorry. Any other last-minute thoughts?"

"Yes. Don't do this."

When Ginny finally saw Brandon yawning, she swooped in and volunteered to escort him back to his car. Though he seemed reluctant to leave at first, at her insistence he finally capitulated and agreed to follow her. Ginny felt a little guilty about forcing the issue, but the suspense was killing her, and his car was really the only place she could think of for a private moment.

To...kiss.

As they silently wended their way through the parking field, she felt positively ill. Beads of sweat broke out on her upper lip and she had to fight back the acid bile that burned in her throat. Nerves. She didn't have a whole lot of experience in this matter, the last years so filled with finishing her education, so she supposed her body was simply in the early phases of excitement over the prospect of kissing Brandon.

That had to be it. She ran a shaky palm over the sheen of sweat on her face and told herself that this was going to be fun. When they reached his car, she turned and awkwardly faced him. The moon was high in the star-filled sky, allowing Ginny to see Brandon quite clearly.

Mentally, she chanted. *Stand close. Be provocative. Look kissable. Stand close. Be provocative. Look kissable.* Suddenly at a loss for the usual end-of-the-evening pleasantries, she blathered another idiotic "Okay then."

"Okay then." His smile was pleasant enough.

"I had a nice time."

"Yep. Me too." Brandon gave his shoulders a genial jerk.

"We should get together again."

Brandon nodded, suddenly distracted by an explosion of hilarity that came from the main tent, where her sisters were flirting with the guys in the band. Rear molars a-grinding, Ginny fought the petulant urge to shake Brandon and force him to pay attention.

Clearly time to implement Colt's advice.

All righty then. First, stand close. As Brandon stared off over his shoulder, Ginny moved in until the toes of their shoes met. Heavens. This seemed a little too close, but she figured Colt was the expert and he'd insisted that standing like this did it for him.

"Maybe a group of us could go out sometime soon."

Brandon spun and reared back, startled to find her face so near to his own. Recovering, he brightened. "A group? That sounds good."

"Okay. I'll…er…call you." She peered up at him. Good heavens. This proximity thing was hardly a turn-on for her. His nostrils seemed huge and his teeth menacing.

"You'll call me," Brandon murmured and arched even farther back, his chin tucked into his neck like a chicken preparing to peck. "All right. That's fine."

"I'll call *before* midnight this time." She forced some laughter.

"Sure." Another blast of frivolity from the tent had Brandon craning yet again after her shrieking sisters. He seemed positively riveted by their folderol. She swallowed her irritation.

"Okay then."

This was not working out at all the way she'd planned. Ginny wracked her brain for Colt's advice. *Drape yourself provocatively against the car,* he'd said.

Seemed idiotic, but hey, whatever worked on the male psyche. While Brandon stared after the party under the big top, Ginny fluffed her hair, plumped her cleavage, pinched her cheeks, licked her lips, popped a breath mint, and then, after positioning her arms just so, draped herself in her most alluring pose against his car door.

It took Ginny a moment to register that the earsplitting shrieks of protest came from Brandon's car alarm. Stunned, she jumped away and wrung her hands as Brandon finally snapped to his senses and turned off the alarm. Seemed his damn car didn't cater to being touched.

"Sorry about that." Ginny smiled sheepishly.

"No prob." Brandon gave his keys a tidy little spin on his forefinger, and then opened his door in preparation for departure.

No! Don't leave yet! "Uh, Brandon!"

"Hmm?" He turned to face her and propped an arm over the door.

"Good night."

Now or never. Do or die. This was it.

Look kissable.

Ginny moved back into firing range and arranged her lips into what she hoped made an appetizing pucker. She closed her eyes. *Okay, baby. Let's get this over with.*

Nothing.

She squinted through her lashes, and her heart fell to her stomach where it lay, quivering.

Brandon shifted his puzzled gaze from her lips, to her eyes, and then back to her lips. His eyebrows arched and his eyes widened.

Time seemed to suspend.

He looked bewildered. Ginny could feel a tiny bead of ice-cold sweat trickle down her spine. Clearly, he had not planned for a good-night kiss at this juncture. Of course. He was right. It was far too soon.

How completely humiliating.

Plan B, her brain screamed. Reverse the engines!

Seeming to realize his breach in etiquette, Brandon puckered and leaned forward as Ginny reared back.

They laughed uncomfortably. She took a step to the side. He did, too. She lowered her arms. Misreading her cues, he lowered his arms and they collided. More strained laughter. Finally she offered her cheek and he quickly pecked it.

They sprang apart.

Good enough, Ginny thought, noting that there had been zero zing from that little kiss. But it was a start. The zing would follow.

"Okay then. I'll call you tomorrow." If she wasn't absolutely convinced that her years of research on the failure rate of attraction-only based relationships, she would be sorely tempted to give up on Brandon. But she simply could not argue with cold, hard facts. Statistically speaking, Brandon was her obvious choice for a marriage with little chance of failure. And Ginny was not one to fail.

Not wanting to be alone with her depressing thoughts, Ginny returned to the party. She hovered at the entrance to the main tent and watched her sisters learn to play the drums and the guitar by candlelight. Yards of white canvas and mosquito netting flapped in the night breeze. The whole scene had a surreal quality. Perhaps that was because she had died of embarrassment and was simply having an out-of-body experience.

A low groan gurgled in her throat as she sighed.

The easygoing musicians leaned over her sisters, giving some impromptu instruction. Though she considered joining them, intrinsically, Ginny knew she'd never fit in. The thought compounded her depression.

Without even turning around, she could sense Colt's lazy approach. His voice rumbled low, over her shoulder. "That first kiss is always the toughest, huh?"

"What, were you spying on me?"

"Nah." He took a toothpick from between his teeth and peered into her face. "You just don't look as if you've been properly kissed."

"And just how would that look?" she snapped.

"Not like you'd been sucking lemons."

She forced herself to relax her facial muscles, hating his knowing tone. "For your information, it wasn't Brandon's fault. I simply sent out the wrong signals. It's way too early for a first kiss."

"Not in my book."

"Oh, so you just grab the woman and...and..." Ginny groped for the verbal image. "Ravage her lips right on the first date?"

"If we had chemistry, I'd kiss her, yeah." He eyed her lazily and she felt her heart begin to pound.

"Chemistry?"

"Yeah, you know, sweaty palms—"

As unobtrusively as possible, Ginny wiped her suddenly clammy hands on her pants.

"Dry mouth."

She swallowed.

"Pounding heart, light head, clenched gut, you know the routine."

"Uh...huh." Wasn't that what she'd felt with Brandon? No, that had been more like the stomach flu. Or perhaps the later stages of the bubonic plague. On the other hand, what she was feeling right now was completely different.

Interesting.

Colt took a step that brought them face-to-face. "Those are the signs I use to determine if a kiss is warranted."

"Oh." The word came out on a little sigh as she blinked up at him.

"So. You said you were sending out some kind of mixed signals? What were you doing wrong?"

"I'm not gonna tell you what I was doing out there with Brandon."

"Why not? Maybe I can help. Give you a few pointers."

Ginny considered his offer. It was true, he probably had a boatload of experience under his belt, to kiss the way he did. And she was certainly an abysmal failure on her own.

"All right then. If you must know, I did…this." She felt the flames of mortification lick her cheeks as she forced herself to pucker up and lean toward Colt.

Colt was so still for so long, she was beginning to fear she'd bored him to tears. Two for two. "That bad, huh?"

"Uh—" He rimmed his lips with his tongue. "No, no," came his hasty assurance. "You're fine. I'm…just…trying to figure out why he didn't kiss you."

"Probably because I look like a dork."

"Honey, you look…beautiful."

Drawing her full lower lip between her teeth, Ginny nervously gnawed. "Then why didn't he kiss me?"

"Don't have a clue. I'm not in his head. If it had been me, I'd have—" his eyelids fell to half mast as he slid his hands around her waist "—pulled you close. Like this."

He leaned against a sturdy tent pole for balance and then, as easily as falling off a wild mustang, he drew her up against his body and folded his arms across her back.

Ginny shivered. No sign of nausea. Only the completely thrilling thrum of her heart. Every nerve ending in her body was on red alert, every sense in hyperdrive as she melted into Colt's enveloping frame.

Mmm.

He smelled so good. Like those dryer sheets with the

little bear on the box. And his breath, coming in warm puffs against her cheeks, smelled slightly of micro-brewed beer and after-dinner peppermints.

His body was warm in the twilight breeze and she could feel the power radiating from him as they stood in the shadows of the tent's entrance. With one hand, he cupped the back of her head and angled it so that he could look directly into her eyes.

"Then I'd have kissed you just once, like this." He bent forward and allowed his lips the briefest of contact and, pulling back, let them hover over hers. "Then, if you leaned into me, the way you are now, with your mouth half-open and your eyes half-closed, I'd do it again."

Colt dipped his head again for a kiss so exquisitely tender and talented that Ginny feared she'd lost con-sciousness. Never before had she ever felt anything like this. And she was up to speed on her emotions. Had a doctorate to prove it. But this? Good heavens. *This* had never been taught in school. Billy Payne and the paltry handful of boys that had slobbered on her in their boy-ish ways had never had such…finesse. Such savoir faire. Such raw, sexual genius. The man was…he was…

He was kissing her jaw, her throat, her nape, her ear. He was lavishing attention on her lower lip, nibbling, teasing and then kissing her with such force and desire that Ginny couldn't breathe.

And she didn't care.

She didn't need to breathe. Not when Colt was hold-ing her this way, breathing for her. Breathing life into her rather shriveled and puny heart.

So. This is what all the fuss was about.

Dreamily, Ginny pressed closer to Colt, loving

these new feelings, reveling in the mysterious connection that seemed to fuse them into one at the lips. Lacing her hands at the nape of his neck, she arched back, giving him room to explore her throat. She shivered from head to toe with the most delicious sensations. Her breath was coming in jagged little puffs, and blood coursed through her body and pounded in her ears. Her knee joints wobbled and she clung to Colt for balance.

Funny how clinging to Colt and gasping his name in a guttural fashion seemed the most natural thing in the world. He'd threaded his fingers through her hair and was cradling her head, plundering her mouth, pillaging her throat, ravaging that little hollow between her collarbones.

It was positively primeval.

She loved it.

Her arms slipped from his neck and rested on his shoulders, and she lay in his solid embrace, a tingling rag doll at the mercy of his amazing gift.

Slowly, Colt set her upright and—after kissing her one last, lingering time—he took a step back and raked a hand over the back of his neck.

"And so that's your answer." His voice was steady but his breathing was still a tad labored. "If you'd looked at me like that, and I was Brandon, I'd have kissed you. Just like that."

"Oh." Dazed, Ginny stared up at him. "Thanks. That was…that was…"

"I know." Colt pushed off the tent pole and grinned. "Educational. You take instruction beautifully." He held out his hand. "C'mon, I'll walk you back to the house."

He escorted her across the lawn and up to the mansion's sprawling front porch in silence.

Off in the distance, Big Daddy was bellowing good-bye to the stragglers. The cleanup crew pulled down tents and folded the tables and chairs. As if on cue, party-rental trucks began to lumber down the driveway to clear everything away. Only the musicians remained, still jamming with Georgia and Carolina, who hadn't a musical bone in their curvy bodies. Nobody seemed to care.

Colt perched on the porch railing, his heel hitched behind a balustrade. "I had fun tonight. You have a great voice."

Ginny ducked her head and murmured, "Thanks. You want to go on a group outing with me and Brandon this week?"

Colt sat, silent. Staring. Finally, "Why?"

"I don't want to date all by myself yet."

Colt grunted in disgust. "You need a chaperon? With a guy who won't kiss you good-night?"

"No, I just—"

"Okay, okay, you don't need to twist my arm. I'll go."

"Gee, thanks."

"Call me tomorrow. Better yet, call me tonight, before you go to sleep."

"Why?"

"So I know you made it safely upstairs."

How typical of Colt. Funny. Sweet. Endearing. Pigheaded. "Okay."

There was a long, self-conscious moment as Ginny willed Colt to move across the porch and take her in his arms for another lesson.

He didn't move. Just sat there. Staring.

She supposed he figured he'd done all he could for her. Slowly she trailed a forefinger across the kiss that still burned on her lower lip and then touched her cheeks, which were slightly raw from the abrasion of his day's growth of whiskers.

She wanted more.

Clearly, he wasn't going to give it.

"Good night, Ginny." With a little salute, Colt sprang off the railing and ambled down the front steps.

"'Night." Suddenly bereft, Ginny watched him stroll to the parking lot, jump into the Durango and disappear into the night. She leaned against a giant Georgian column as the dust on the road slowly settled in Colt's wake.

Umm, she exhaled, *hmm.*

Wooing Brandon McGraw was going to take a lot more emotional energy than she'd counted on.

The next morning, Ginny rose and dressed after a fitful sleep. Plagued by endless, fragmented dreams, she'd tossed and turned until the sun rose above the distant mountains. All night she and Colt had been riding a lawn mower down long corridors in hot pursuit of Brandon. Then they were running. All the while, her legs were made of jelly, and try as she might to keep up with Colt, he was always just out of reach until he turned magically—and quite naturally—into Carolina, who held out her cell phone.

"It's Brandon," Carolina said. "For you."

"Kiss me," Ginny shrieked into the phone and then threw it away when Brandon suddenly appeared. "Brandon! Dammit! *Kiss me!*" But, try as she might to capture his attention, with Irish clog dancing and bubble blowing, he was lured away by the music.

"Stop him!" she shouted at Colt, who was no longer Carolina. "I have to kiss him, don't you see? It's the only way…the only way…"

But instead of following Brandon, Colt dropped to his knee, slipped a ring from a gumball machine on her finger and said, "Denial is a river in Egypt."

And then she'd woken up.

Okay. Ginny scratched her head. That one would take some serious analysis. Deciding that perhaps getting out of the house might help clear the cobwebs, she went downstairs and tapped lightly on Miss Clarise's office door.

"C'mon in, it's open," came the soft invitation.

Miss Clarise, looking fresh as a daisy after last night's party, was busily arranging her daily schedule over the phone, with her personal assistant. Covering the mouthpiece with her delicate hand, she waved Ginny to come sit in one of the two Queen Anne chairs positioned directly in front of her desk.

As she complied, Ginny's gaze wandered about the beautifully appointed office. Though the decor was rich and feminine, there was also a no-nonsense, business-like quality evident in very subtle ways. On the wall hung a picture of Miss Clarise posing with the first lady, accepting an award for her advocation and generous funding of children's literacy programs. Next to the picture hung that award. And Ginny knew what was contained in those two frames represented a plethora of generous and charitable work that would never even be acknowledged by her aunt.

Miss Clarise made several concise notes on her calendar, then hung up and turned to face her niece.

"Hi, darlin'. What can I do for you this mornin'?"

Ginny smoothed her skirt over her knees. "Well, I was wondering if it would be all right if I borrowed a car and ran into town for a few personal things."

Last night, Carolina and Georgia had absconded with most of her toiletries and makeup. Plus, after perusing the movie selection in her parlor, Ginny decided that, since her tastes were in no way represented, a trip to the video store would be in order.

"I hate to ask, but my sisters have taken off with the car to have breakfast with some musicians…."

"Say no more, sweetheart." Miss Clarise dialed the ranch offices on her speakerphone. Colt's voice boomed into the room on the second ring.

"Hey, Miss Clarise, what can I do for you?"

At the sound of his mellifluous voice, Ginny's breathing became shallow. She clutched her chair's armrests until her knuckles whitened. Good night nurse, she thought as she tried to rein in her runaway pulse, her response was positively Pavlovian. What the devil was wrong with her?

"Colt, darlin', I want you to bring a rig up for Ginny. She needs to run a few errands over in Hidden Valley and would like to leave right away."

"Great. I'll be right up. I have to go to Hidden Valley myself, so I'll drive her."

Ginny started to protest but was cut off by Miss Clarise's enthusiastic reply. "Why, that's wonderful! And much safer that way. Come on up, honey. She'll be out front waiting for you."

Having no recourse, Ginny smiled weakly and then left to gather her purse and shopping list.

Chapter Six

Colt hung up, pleased that he'd be taking Ginny to town. If he had some time alone with her, maybe he could talk her out of this nutty scientific-mating scheme. Feet propped on the corner of his desk, he stretched back and coiled the phone's cord around his finger. Given enough time, he was sure he could convince her to follow her heart when it came to love.

No, ma'am, Colt Bartlett's mama didn't raise no dummy. He could tell that Ginny responded to the physical attraction that sizzled between them as much as he did. She'd wanted more last night. And he'd have given it if he hadn't been trying to teach *her* a lesson. Simply put, Colt's lesson: Brandon boring. Colt exciting.

Family history unimportant.

A small grin crawled across his lips as he remembered how she'd melted against him, offering her mouth, her warm, pliant body. He sobered. Everything but her heart.

He pulled the cord off his finger and, grabbing a yellow pad, drummed up a quick list of veterinary supplies that would make his trip to Hidden Valley's farm supply store seem like one he'd been planning for ages. But it was hard to concentrate. Visions of last night kept the elevator between his mind and belly busy. Her kiss swirled in his mind, shot to his gut, created havoc and then flashed back to his increasingly dazed lump of gray matter.

What a night.

Colt hadn't remembered feeling so exhilarated and glad to simply be alive since... The springs in his chair squeaked as he stared up through the skylight in the ceiling and reviewed his life.

Nah, he'd never felt this alive.

Not even the day he'd first kissed Renee. Nor the day he bought the ring. No, it hadn't even felt this good when Renee had sobbingly accepted his proposal and then proceeded to count the karats in her new diamond.

Ginny Brubaker did amazing things to him. Simply being in the same room with her caused his body temperature to spike and endorphins to torpedo through his brain. It felt plain old good to be with Ginny. Just like it had when they were kids. Only now there was a whole new dynamic.

Her kiss was quickly becoming an obsession for him. And the very idea of sharing her...nearly drove him insane.

Which was a laugh, considering her profession. Colt allowed his head to thud back against the thickly padded headrest. What on earth was he thinking here? Was he falling in love with Ginny Brubaker?

That was a tough question considering he'd loved her

since they used to play in the wading pool together as toddlers. But...*in* love? That was a different thing altogether.

How did one know if one was *in* love? After all, he thought he'd had that with Renee, but come to find out he'd simply been in lust.

Was that what was happening here?

Colt didn't know, but one thing was for sure, something about all this man-hunting subterfuge had his guts roiling. It was just plain wrong, and he needed to keep an eye on Ginny before she got hurt. Plus, it didn't exactly seem fair to old Brandon. Poor guy didn't really even stand a chance against a female with a plan and a doctorate. She and Brandon were a mismatch. Anyone could see that.

Anyone, it seemed, but Ginny.

His feet thudded to the floor, and as he sat up Colt sighed, grabbed the keys to the Durango and headed out the door to take Ginny shopping.

By the time lunch hour rolled around, both Ginny and Colt were ravenous. Because it was across the street from the Farm Grow Store, and because it was too beautiful a day to sit inside, they decided that it would be fun to go to Cheese Louise, a pizza parlor/miniature golf course. Out on a deck festooned with flower baskets and umbrella-clad tables, Ginny and Colt took their seats and groaned. Oh, but it felt good to sit down.

Feeling uncommonly serene, Ginny sat back, enjoying the lively, piped-in Italian music and the light breeze that ruffled her hair. It was shady and cool on this warm summer day and the iced tea that Colt had ordered for them was refreshing. She unfolded her paper napkin and absently began to polish her flatware.

"So. You ever think about falling in love again?" Ginny was surprised to hear herself wonder aloud.

Eyes half mast, Colt leaned back and regarded her with such an enigmatic look that if she had to label it she'd say it was equal parts suspicion and hope.

"I dunno. Why?"

"No reason. I just wondered who might be in your life since your breakup with Renee."

"I've had feelings for someone."

Ginny froze. "You have?"

"Mmm. But I'm not ready to talk about it."

"Feelings, as in…love?"

"You're doing it again."

"What?"

"Prying."

"But—"

"Ginny." His voice held warning.

"Sorry."

In their awkward silence, they stared off beyond the deck and watched families golf through elaborately designed windmills and castles. Children laughed and shouted, parents praised, families bonded.

Ginny longed to be out there with her very own family and tried to picture Brandon and herself with their children, but the visual image wouldn't quite gel. Visions of Colt and his family kept intruding. There was another woman? Who? Fretting, Ginny smoothed out her napkin then folded it into an intricate origami shape and battled an unaccustomed stab of something protective. Not jealousy, of course, but something. She hated any woman who would hurt Colt's feelings and break his sweet heart.

Obviously, considering the Renee travesty, Colt

didn't have the best instincts when it came to finding his soul mate. But then, he was basing his criteria on matters of the heart. Big mistake.

Clearly he needed her professional help. But knowing that he'd never willingly comply with her commonsense approach on his own, Ginny knew she'd have to help him in other ways.

In fact…

Why not?

Suddenly excited, Ginny sat up and stared unseeing at the bird of paradise she'd created out of her napkin as she contemplated her plan. *Yes.*

With the proper testing and a bit of research, *she* could fix him up with a good woman. The right woman. The one most perfectly suited to his particular personality. But first it would be necessary to discover what kind of woman would be right for him. Compatible. Of a like background.

"Colt!"

He jumped, obviously deep in his own thoughts. "What?"

"I want to help you find a woman."

Jaw sagging, Colt simply stared. "Come again?"

"Using my plan, silly. I want to help you find the woman most compatible to your—"

A long groan rumbled from the back of his throat. "No! You know I don't believe—"

"Right, right. What is it you believe again?"

"Call me old-fashioned, but I believe a man and a woman simply fall in love. Love will help them conquer whatever differences they might face."

Ginny guffawed as she bent to tug her purse up into her lap. "What about when love dies?"

"Love is something you have to work at. Every day. It's like a job. If you want to keep it bad enough, you'll invest the time."

"How…quaint." Ginny tilted her purse and after a quick, alphabetical scan, extracted a slim file folder. "Anyway, as you are now well aware, it is my belief that if a couple starts out with the same sets of values, goals and beliefs, all the hard work of propping up a failing marriage will never be an issue."

Lacing his fingers across his stomach, Colt crossed his legs at the ankles and settled back for the lecture. "What failing marriage?"

"Don't you remember me telling you about Mr. and Mrs. Smith?"

"Yeah. And I think their problems went way back to being raised like spoiled brats by aging hippies and then trying to play nice together as grown-ups."

"You are entitled to your hypothesis, Doctor." Ginny opened her file and pulled out his answer sheets and the corresponding scorecards.

"Thank you."

"Okay, just for fun and practice, while we're waiting for our food, I'll go over your personality test results from all the tests I gave you and we can find out what kind of woman you should be dating."

Colt snapped a bread stick in two. "How about one I *love?*"

"If you want a bunch of heartache, sure."

"Whatever. Go on."

The food arrived unnoticed by Ginny as she reviewed the battery of questions that Colt and her sisters and cousins had all answered yesterday out at the pond.

Too hungry to wait, Colt dug into his lasagna as

Ginny hmmed and mmmed and made copious notes in the test paper's margins. After fifteen minutes or so, sparks of cerebral energy seemed to crackle the air. Colt watched with interest as she reached for her purse, whipped a calculator from its tidy contents and began figuring percentages with flying fingers.

"Amazing," she murmured, pumping up his curiosity. "This can't be right. I need to recalculate this, hang on a sec."

Colt shrugged and speared a forkful of her pasta. "Sure." The food here wasn't half-bad. Her entrée was delicious. He couldn't believe Ginny wasn't eating.

"Well," she breathed, "will wonders never cease."

He stopped chewing and leaned forward. "What? What?" Though he was loath to admit it, Colt was dying to know what she'd discovered.

"Well, according to my calculations—combined with the hypothesis of my dissertation, where couples who score similarly on a battery of tests are more compat—"

"Ginny, for heaven's sake, get to the point!"

"Okay. Your perfect match—with the lone exception of family background, which I suppose isn't that big of a deal, considering you were raised on the Circle BO—would be my sister Carolina."

A searing pain brought tears to his eyes as Colt swallowed a big bite of bread stick without chewing.

Carolina?

Glancing up, Ginny noted his incredulous expression. "I know! Wild, huh? And this is taking into account the more than three thousand single women I tested over the last two years." Staring off into the past, she stroked her jaw with her thumb and forefinger. "It's amazing that you two weren't inseparable as children."

Not to Colt it wasn't. Surely she had to be kidding. Not that Carolina wasn't cute and all, but she did nothing for him, personality speaking. Except perhaps drive him nuts with all her shenanigans. He'd been tempted to throttle her more than once when they were growing up. He and Carolina? Together as anything but buddies?

Never in a million years.

Carolina was too much of a free spirit. They would never last. He made an attempt at some disbelieving laughter, but his throat was killing him. He reached for his glass of iced tea and guzzled.

Finally he was able to speak. "Are you serious?"

"Perfectly."

"What kind of a quack are you?"

Blithely, Ginny ignored the barb and dug into her salad. "It'll be interesting to finally test Brandon."

"I'm surprised you didn't do that last night."

Ginny rolled her eyes. "When would I have had time? I was too busy…" She blushed. "You know."

"Yeah." He palmed the back of his neck and squeezed. He knew.

Ginny nattered on about Brandon and how, even though things felt "a little awkward," she could tell that there had been potential there last night. She just needed to spend more time getting acquainted.

Potential. What a load of bull.

Colt knew that he and Ginny had both nearly gone up in flames last night during the kiss they'd shared in the shadow of the tent. And he knew that she knew it. Talk about denial. *Physician, heal thyself,* he wanted to shout. Even after only two lousy psychology classes in college, even *he* could see that she was repressing her true feelings in favor of some nebulous ideal.

Such a waste.

Such a damn pathetic waste.

In his peripheral vision, Colt watched Ginny's slender hand ride the air currents out the passenger window as he drove them home. Soft jazz filled the cab, creating a mellow mood as the scenery came and went. A tinfoil swan containing Ginny's half-eaten pasta perched beside a package of cosmetics and toiletries they'd shopped for at the pharmacy. The colognes she'd tried on there tickled his senses, heightening his awareness of her.

Refocusing on the road, Colt knew she was deep in thought over his test results. The cool breeze from the window lifted her hair and blew strands across her face and lips. He resisted the urge to reach out and tuck them behind her ear.

After a moment, she turned and bestowed a smile upon him.

"I want to invite Brandon over on Saturday to go horseback riding with you and me and Carolina."

"Carolina? Is this gonna be like a date? Cuz you're not thinking about setting me up with your sister, are you?"

"You two are compatible."

"Sure are. According to the books, we're practically made for each other. Should probably skip the preliminaries and go straight to the altar."

"Oh no you don't! I mean, I'm not suggesting you marry her or anything."

"Why not? Is it because I'm from the wrong side of the tracks?"

Ginny lifted an unamused eyebrow. "Just go for a ride with her. And me. And Brandon. We'll double date.

You take care of the horses and I'll take care of getting us some lunch."

Colt couldn't help but grin at her, even though he knew the date would be disastrous all the way around.

She returned his smile, taking it as a sign of acquiescence. "A double date it is, then. Fun."

Sure. But only if Brandon and Carolina stayed home.

Immersed in his work, the rest of the week flew by for Colt. He and Hank and Kenny had dinner with the girls every night. Then the six of them would play horseshoes or darts or pool until dark, when they'd crawl into the hot tub and yak till well past midnight.

Colt couldn't be sure how Ginny felt, as they were never alone, but he could barely be in the same room with her without feeling as if he were going to explode from this unexpected physical attraction. It was making him crazy. Keeping him awake at night, messing with his head. Her endless prattle about Brandon didn't help matters any.

And now, well, now it was bright and early Saturday morning and he had a date with Ginny's sister. Super.

The horses had been fed, watered, curried, saddled and were tethered and at the ready. He'd showered, shampooed and shaved and jumped into his newest blue jeans, a fresh T-shirt and his most comfortable pair of riding boots. He was packed and ready to go and it was still an hour before Ginny expected him. *Them.*

Tired of pacing his tiny living room, he grabbed a travel mug of coffee, waved at Kenny who was only just now stumbling out of bed, and headed for the Durango.

Happily, Ginny must have been equally unable to rest, for she was sitting on the porch steps nursing her own cup of coffee as he drove up and parked.

"Hey," he called as he strolled up to join her.

"Hey yourself." She scooted over a bit to make room for him in a shady patch. "I'm glad you came early."

Slowly he lowered himself to her side. "Uh-oh. Why?" He looked askance at her over the rim of his mug and felt the blood pick up speed in his veins. Have mercy, it was hard to sit this close to her without wanting to do something stupid.

"I was hoping you could make Brandon feel comfortable today."

"Comfortable?"

"Yes. I don't think he gets out of the office to ride much, so he's—"

"Sissified."

"No!"

"And you want me to hold his hand?"

Ginny sighed. "Why not? You're Mr. Dude Ranch, right?"

Colt winced. Aw, criminy sakes, he didn't want to be a party to this mess. Then he made the terrible mistake of meeting her gaze, and her hopeful expression was all it took. He was a hapless booby when it came to denying her anything. Always had been.

Elbows to knees, he hunched forward and sighed into his coffee mug. "Sure. What the heck. I'll help out where I can."

She stared at him, long and hard. "I want this to go well today, Colt," she warned.

"It will. Relax."

"Okay." There was a dubious quality to her voice. With a sigh, Ginny smoothed the nonexistent wrinkles in her perfectly pressed khaki slacks, then patted her upswept hair and straightened her collar, licked her lips, swallowed and started over again.

By the time Brandon finally arrived, Ginny was as nervous as a goldfish in a toilet bowl. By comparison, Carolina was relaxed and charming, making Ginny come off like a social totem pole as they all strolled toward the barn together to gather the horses.

Colt stayed several paces behind everyone, mainly to observe what the heck it was that Ginny saw in this Brandon doorknob. It was evident from the get-go that he was more comfortable shooting the breeze with the effervescent Carolina than with the suddenly tongue-tied Ginny.

That irritated Colt. The least Mr. Fancy-pants could do would be to make an effort to indulge in some small talk with his date. Colt's mama had taught him that much back when he was still in short pants.

Nevertheless, looking as if he'd just stepped off the pages of *Gentleman's Quarterly,* on the outside Brandon seemed the perfect counterpart to Ginny, and for a moment Colt struggled with doubt. Maybe Ginny was right. Maybe they were supposed to be together.

Suddenly Colt felt like some dumb cowpuncher with a bad haircut. No wonder he'd never made it to Ginny's list.

Forcing himself to shrug off his funk, Colt moved ahead and led the little group into the barn. Here the air was cool and smelled of freshly strewn hay. A wide hallway lined with stalls contained champion horseflesh of all breeds. Curious nickers welcomed them as they passed, to come and give a carrot or two.

Once they reached the paddock out back, Colt assigned the horses. According to Ginny's wishes, he helped Brandon discover which end of the horse went giddyup and then swung into his own saddle, glad at least to be on his own turf. In his comfort zone. He'd been born in a saddle and in that respect anyway he had the edge over the more dignified Brandon.

As they left the paddock and hit the open road leading through Big Daddy's massive oil fields, it seemed to Colt that no matter how hard Ginny tried to lob Brandon the conversational ball, he would smash it into the net, where it would roll pointlessly in his court. On the other hand, never at a loss for words, Carolina would casually toss out a topic that would pull old Brandon back into the game.

Interesting.

Twisting in her saddle, Ginny shot a beseeching look at Colt, urging him with her eyes to say something, anything, to kick-start the conversation in her favor.

And Colt simply couldn't resist the demons that drove him to respond.

"So, Brandon," Colt called as he rode up behind them, "read any good books lately?"

Brandon shrugged, taken back. "Uh…I…no."

"Ah." Colt nodded. "Ginny likes to read, doncha, Gin?"

"Yes."

"So, Brandon," Colt persisted, "seen any good art house films lately?"

"No."

"Ginny loves all those weird, subtitled things that always end miserably. Yeah, she also enjoys a fine cigar and sitting on duck eggs. Did it for days on end back when we were kids. Did everything together back then. Yep…everything. I've seen her naked."

Ginny emitted some strangled laughter. "He's kidding, Brandon." She waved Colt away with a rude gesture behind her.

Carolina dropped back beside Colt and he flashed her a grin as they plodded along side by side.

"You'd better cool it," Carolina advised in a low tone. "I think I can see the thunderclouds forming over her head."

"What? No way. Look at her. She's smiling."

"Yeah. Means she's gonna kill you later. You should know that by now."

Colt gave his shoulder a careless lift. "I was just trying to get things started."

"No you weren't."

"Okay. No I wasn't."

Her smile small and knowing, Carolina stared at Colt so long he began to wonder if he'd sprouted a third eye.

The high-pitched whine of grasshoppers' song and the jangle and squeak of horse rigging serenaded them as they clip-clopped down the dirt road. Swirls of dust fairly obliterated Ginny and Brandon from sight and forced Colt and Carolina to drop even farther back. Carolina's stare never wavered.

Colt glanced at her smug expression and shrugged. "What?"

"You're in love with her, aren't you?"

"What?" Colt's heart lodged in his throat. What was she asking? Was he in love with Ginny? And if he was, was he that transparent? "I...I...come again?"

Carolina nudged her mount so close their stirrups touched. Heads together, she whispered as they rode, "You. You're in love. With my sister. The doctor."

"What the Sam Hill makes you say that?"

"I knew it back when we were little kids, but I can see by the look deep in your eyes that nothing has changed."

"I loved her when we were little, yeah. She was the closest thing I had to a sibling."

"*In* love. You were *in* love then. You are now."

"You're crazy."

Ginny and Brandon glanced back over their shoulders and waved. Colt and Carolina paused long enough to return the salute then continued in hushed whispers.

"*In* love. What is *in* love?" Colt asked.

"It's what you are with Ginny. The way she makes you feel. As if you don't want to live without her. Can't live without her. The difference between living and simply existing. The difference between happiness and—" Carolina inclined her head at her sister and Brandon "—that."

Wrists crossed at his saddle horn, Colt fell silent for a long, long time. "Okay. Maybe."

"No maybe. It's *luuuuuvvvve,* honey. And you've got it bad. Poor baby."

"So. I'm that transparent."

"'Fraid so, bucko. And one of the reasons I'm so sure is that I—" nose wrinkled, Carolina's tone was self-deprecating "—recognize the feelings in myself."

"You have an unrequited crush on someone?"

Carolina nodded at Brandon's back.

Colt frowned. "Pardon?"

"Brandon."

"You're hung up on Brandon? Brandon McGraw? *That*—" he pointed "—Brandon McGraw?"

"Shh!" Carolina slapped at his pointing finger. "Yes, *that* Brandon McGraw. Who else could I be talking about?"

Colt threw back his head and laughed. "Oh, this is rich. How do you suppose your sister would explain this?"

"I don't know, but it wouldn't be English."

They enjoyed the humor born of irony.

Attracted by the fun, Ginny glanced back, her smile wistful.

Carolina lowered her voice. "As Ginny told you, we met Brandon for the first time since we were kids at a Christmas party two years ago, although he seemed to pay more attention to Georgia than anyone. But I haven't been able to stop thinking about him since. I've been wracked with guilt knowing how Ginny feels about him. Aren't I terrible?" A rueful grin twisted Carolina's lips. "What a couple of losers we are."

Colt shrugged. "You can't help how you feel. Feelings are just that. Feelings. They're not good or bad. They just are."

"Man, you sound like Ginny."

"Yeah. She's rubbing off on me. Anyway you do understand that your sister had us come along for several reasons?"

"And those are?"

"Well, for one, she does not want to be alone with tall, dark and playboy up there."

"He's not like that, really."

Colt jerked a shoulder. "Yeah, yeah. And two, she's hoping that you and I will get together for a little harmless summer romance."

"She *is?*"

"Yup. According to the tests we took, you and I are a match made in heaven."

Carolina's mouth fell open and incredulous laughter gurgled forth. "You? Me? Oh, that's hysterical."

Eyebrows beetled, Colt could only stare. "What am I that all of you Brubaker girls see me as some kind of eunuch?"

"No!" she hastened to assure him. "I don't. I see you as Ginny's soul mate."

"You do?"

"Yep. Always have. Ever since you two sat on those rotten eggs for a week solid, we all thought there are two nuts from the same fruitcake. So—" Carolina eyed him speculatively "—what should we do?"

"Well, you know, I've been giving that some thought and I think we should give her a taste of her own medicine."

"Meaning?"

Colt reached out and took her hand and let their arms swing between the horses' bodies. "I think we should take Ginny up on her test results and fall head over heels in love."

"Really?" Carolina's face twisted into a perplexed knot.

"No." Colt grabbed his hat with his free hand and slapped it on his thigh to rid it of dust. Clapping it back on his head, he leaned toward Carolina. "Of course not really, you goose. We just want them to think that."

"Why?"

"Because I think a little jealousy may go a long way."

"You want to make them jealous?"

"Why not?"

After a moment's thought, the mirth started in Carolina's belly and exploded past her lips. "You are brilliant!" Riding a little closer, she tugged Colt's arm and planted a kiss on his cheek.

Chapter Seven

Brandon McGraw had one of those voices that could soothe even the most dedicated insomniac to sleep. Try as she might, Ginny was having a heck of a time keeping up with the gist here. What the devil was he droning on about now? It seemed he had one of those careers that even when you knew what he did for a living, you still didn't know. Her head throbbed from the strain.

Behind her she could hear Colt and Carolina yukking it up about something or other. Suddenly she wished she were riding back there. Sounded as if they were having fun.

Ginny dragged a palm over her upper lip. Man it was hot out here. Her wilted clothes were covered with dust, and she could feel the grit in her teeth. All around her, grasshoppers sprang out of the grass, irritated by the swirling dirt the horses kicked up in passing. The horses shook their heads and blew noisily through their nostrils.

Ahead, the road loomed endlessly.

Above, the sun beat mercilessly.

Beside her, Brandon droned incessantly.

Whose brainy idea had this been, anyway?

She licked her lips and redoubled her effort to concentrate on Brandon's nattering. Wasn't it something about U.S. tax provisions and restrictive land access policies? Gracious. She was a Ph.D. Surely she could follow his lines of reasoning. If only she weren't so interested in what was going on behind her.

"—our nation's domestic production capacity and infrastructure are stretched to the limit. A comprehensive national energy policy that encourages international investment—"

"Mmm, hmm." What were Colt and Carolina finding so fascinating back there? It was driving her nuts, not knowing.

"—and world energy demand will be more than sixty percent higher and it is expected that three-quarters of that energy demand growth index—"

Ginny nodded, not registering a word. "Uh-huh."

Unable to resist temptation, she stole another quick peek over her shoulder. Colt really did look good with Carolina. Her test results were...

Were they holding hands?

Bathed in a sudden cold sweat, Ginny grabbed the pommel of her saddle and hung on for dear life. She felt dizzy. Faint.

Could it be the beginning signs of sunstroke? she wondered.

It *was* horribly hot out here.

Certainly she was not this disoriented and confused because her sister was simply holding hands with her best buddy. No. After all, she'd been the one to encourage their romance.

Must be the heat. She reached for her water bottle and took a long, chilling drink. They sure were having a good time back there.

Ginny swabbed her face with her neckerchief and batted at a bug that plagued her.

"—international tax rules are quite complex and expose multinational companies to potential—"

A blast of laughter came from behind.

She dabbed at her forehead. Funny, before she'd tested them, she never would have put those two together in a million years. But you couldn't argue with science. Even so, out of all the people in her family, she'd have thought that Colt would have tested more compatibly with…well, with her. Probably because they got on so well as children.

"—transportation and distribution system that ensures that there will be enough of our industry's—"

Hopefully, Brandon would test so compatibly with her, this whole torturous, "getting to know you" phase would seem worthwhile.

His grin a Texas mile wide, Colt plotted with Carolina. She had a knack for considering all the angles and he could hardly wait to implement their plan.

"—that," she continued in a hushed voice, "will keep 'em guessing and we won't appear to be pining away after them. And, at the same time, we can keep an eye on 'em and see where things might be heading. *Plus*—" Carolina gave her hands an excited flapping "—and this is the best part—if all goes well, I think our mushy little scheme will make us seem sexy."

"I love it." He did. It was brilliant. "They'll eventually have to come to their senses. When they do, we'll be there to catch 'em when they fall. And if they don't eventually break up, at least we'll have each other's shoulders to cry on."

"Great." Carolina nodded. "When should we start?"

"I don't know. How 'bout now?"

"Okay." Fingers still twined, they shook in agreement.

"Laugh," Carolina instructed.

"Now?"

"Yes. Really loud."

Colt shrugged and emitted some thigh-slapping hoots. "So. Tell me. What was so funny?"

"Nothing. You find me amusing, that's all."

"Roger."

"Okay, now lean toward me and hang on my every word."

"Ten-four."

"Now, reach up and touch my hair."

Eyes closed, Colt pretended it was Ginny, whose flyaway strands he tenderly tucked behind her ear.

"Good. Good. They're looking."

"Yeah. They look a little bored with each other."

"Excellent. Laugh."

Colt hardy-harred at the broad Texas sky and Carolina joined in with a tinkling lilt that provided just the right harmony.

"Good," she murmured. "I must be funny."

"Looking."

"Oh," she cried for Brandon's benefit, "you are such a flirt, Colt Bartlett. You say the cutest things."

"So do you, pooh-doodle."

"Okay, sugar-booger, listen up." She lowered her voice. "Here's another thought. We try to double date with Brandon and Ginny as often as possible so that they won't have much time alone. Capiche? Then we figure out ways to undermine their relationship with well-meaning yet subtly derogatory comments."

"You are dastardly."

"I try," Carolina simpered.

"Give me an example so we're on the same page."

"Well, when you're alone with Ginny, say stuff like, 'That Brandon seems like a really neat guy, for a wuss.' And I'll say stuff to Brandon like, 'My sister is so carefree now that she's worked through her fear of abandonment issues. She used to be a real clinging vine.'"

Colt scratched his jaw. "I think I'm getting the hang of it. How about this? 'They said those anger management classes Brandon had to take back when we were in grade school together wouldn't work, but as far as I know, he hasn't vandalized anything for years.'"

Carolina stared at him in admiration. "Oh, you are so good! And I'll tell Brandon that Ginny is super worried about her biological clock losing the race against time. Especially since she wants to have more children than our folks did."

Sobering, Colt raised an eyebrow. "Does she?"

"No!"

"Thank God. You tell Brandon that she wants to name all the kids after…uh…famous psychiatrists. Little Sigmund and Hermann will be the firstborn."

"Even if they are girls?"

"Especially if they are girls."

The next afternoon, as they all stood on the front steps of the quaint country church the Brubaker family attended, Ginny invited her sisters to join her on a shopping trip, as she wanted to buy a new outfit. Something a little more daring and sophisticated than the practical clothes she'd brought from home. Last night she and Brandon had made a date for next Saturday night. Dinner. And perhaps a movie.

Ginny wasn't feeling all that confident about the idea of spending an entire evening all alone with Brandon yet, but figured at the very least it would be a character-building experience.

"We'd love to, sis," Georgia said, "but we're taking a road trip to visit some old classmates and won't be back until late this afternoon."

"Oh." Ginny was disappointed. "Never mind. I can go by myself."

"No such thing," Carolina declared in her best Southern belle voice, and pulled Colt to her side. "You can borrow my honey. That okay with you, Colt, darlin'?"

"Anything, punkin' pie."

Ginny waved a dismissive hand. "That's okay. Never mind. Really. I was going clothes shopping. Brandon asked me out for a date this Saturday night."

"He did?" Colt shot Carolina a loaded glance. "Then we'll double! Just the four of us. It'll be a hoot."

"But...but..." As much as Ginny preferred not to be alone with Brandon, she knew that eventually they were going to have to take that particular plunge. Then again, perhaps another double date would bring him out of his shell. Confusion had her nodding in acquiescence. "Okay. I guess that will be all right. We were going to dinner and a movie."

"What a coincidence!" Colt crowed. "Us, too!"

Carolina pushed her face into his sleeve and shook with laughter.

Colt petted and scratched her head as if she were a golden retriever. "You know, Carolina honey, I want to look my best for you, too. Maybe I should go to the mall and pick me up some new threads. What's your favorite color, my little pork rib?"

"Anything neon?" Carolina shrugged.

Adam's apple bobbing, Colt grimaced. "Then neon it is!"

"Get something for me, too?"

"Of course."

"Neon?" Ginny stared at him. "Since when do you wear neon?"

"Since you made it clear that your sister is my soul mate, that's when. C'mon." Colt took Ginny's hand. "Let's go. I wanna buy lunch for my future sister-in-law."

Carolina's foolish giggles were the fingernails on the chalkboard that brought on Ginny's sudden headache as she followed Colt to his SUV.

But it was too late to back out now.

Mall music echoed in the giant food court that sported three solid stories of junk food around an Olympic-size ice rink. Shoppers bustled hither and thither, lugging packages and strollers and screaming children. Teenagers cruised by surveying the available dating pool and conversing loudly in their own special language.

Off in a little courtyard, Colt and Ginny ate hamburgers and sipped lemonade as they geared up for round two: shopping for Ginny.

Ginny lipped her straw and watched Colt eat. He

was actually going to wear that gaudy Hawaiian-print shirt for Carolina this Saturday night? She'd never seen him in anything other than an assortment of black, white and gray T-shirts. And now this?

"You and Carolina seemed to be getting on like a house on fire." She offered him a bright smile and hoped her irritation didn't show.

"Oh, yeah. I think your tests must be right. She is really the one for me. No question."

Ginny's heart lodged in her throat. "None? After spending only one afternoon together?"

"Can't argue with the numbers. You said that yourself, I believe."

Wanting to kick herself for making such bold statements in front of a layperson, Ginny composed her face into that of a professional. "Well, yes, but I still believe that one should take time to get to *know* that person before one falls in love."

"Why? We have the test scores. What more does 'one' need?"

As Ginny stared at him, she had to wonder at the emotions that suddenly detonated in her belly. Colt and Carolina? Together? So *soon?* Why did this give her such a feeling of…of…foreboding? It was much too soon for something like that.

Never mind. She should be focusing this energy on her own relationship with Brandon. However, the delight of a day spent shopping at the mall with her buddy, Colt, was suddenly gone. For some reason, Colt's announcement had largely taken the wind out of her sails.

No longer hungry, she pushed her burger back. "You ready to hit the stores?"

"You betcha."

* * *

Ginny slipped in and out of the women's fitting room while Colt drummed his fingers on the chair. Women. What on earth was so fascinating about trying on every dad-blamed outfit in the store? It had taken him less than ten minutes total to find his and Carolina's garish shirts, plunk down his money and leave. Yet it seemed Ginny wasn't going to budge from this stupid boutique until she found just the outfit that would have old Brandon-boy drooling in his shoes.

Well, he'd be damned if he'd help her do that.

"What about this outfit?" Ginny wondered as she skipped out of the dressing room in a pair of flowered pedal pushers.

Colt swallowed. He loved how they clung to her figure. The color was perfect. "I hate it. Too tight. Makes you look sickly."

"Really? Oh. Can't have that."

Can't have that, he mouthed sourly as she retreated *back* to the dressing room. When she emerged again, she was wearing a short skirt with matching sweater set.

"It exposes far too much thigh. Makes you look kinda rectangular," is all he would offer on the skirt that showed her legs off to perfection.

"Rectangular?" Ginny frowned.

"Yeah. Square. Only longer."

Rather deflated, Ginny headed back and donned a little sleeveless sundress that was cut low at the neckline, exposing her cleavage.

As much as Colt loved Ginny in this outfit, he saw red when he thought about her showing off her lush attributes to Brandon.

She twirled in front of the trifold mirror. "How about this one? It's casual but elegant."

"What elegant? Don't you think it's kind of trampy?"

"Trampy?"

"Your arms are bare."

She stared, incredulous. "So?"

"Go cover them up. Long sleeves are in."

"But it will be hot out there."

"It won't be that hot. We're going out to dinner and a movie, for crying out loud. It will be air-conditioned."

"Yes, but that's not until Saturday. What about tonight?"

"To—" Colt felt as if someone had crammed an old sweat sock down his throat "—*night?* You are going out with Brandon tonight? Nobody told me."

"I didn't know we had to check in with you," she said dryly. "Besides, we're not going *out,* exactly. Tonight Brandon is coming over to go for a walk through the rose garden."

"A walking date."

"Yeah."

"With Brandon?"

"Yes."

"Then you'll need some boots."

"Colt, we are strolling through the rose garden not climbing Mount Everest."

"You don't want to get a blister."

"I don't think there is much danger of that." Ginny leaned against the three-way dressing mirror and folded her arms under her breasts, plumping her cleavage to interesting proportions. Colt was dazzled. In triplicate. "After the walk, I thought I'd administer some tests over dessert. Try to get a handle on our compatibility level."

"Ah. The all-knowing inkblot tests."

"Yes. Anyway, I've been thinking and hoping that to-night, while we are on our walk, you could, you know, be around, so that we might 'run into' you. And then you could mention to Brandon that you'd like to join us Saturday night?"

"Why don't you just tell him that plans have changed and we're all going together?"

"Because I don't want him to think that I don't want to be alone with him."

"Don't you?"

"Please, Colt. Just do it. Make it seem spur of the moment."

Marshaling his powers of concentration, Colt tore his gaze from the creamy flesh of the bustline that strained against the little sundress she wore and focused on her hopeful eyes.

He dropped his head in his hands and groaned. "You'll have to tell me exactly what time I'm supposed to 'pass through,' so that I won't be 'passing through' for an hour."

"Then you'll do it?"

Ginny's bright expression tugged at what little was left of his bleeding heart. He never could resist her when she pleaded with him this way.

"And you *promise* not to embarrass me this time."

"I…promise."

"Oh, thank you, Colt. I'm really glad we'll be doubling with you. I really didn't want the entire burden of conversation to rest on my shoulders."

"Why not? That's what dating is all about. You talk. He talks. You stop talking. He stops talking. The tortured conversation lags into one big cesspool of boredom. But hey, that's just part of the dang fun."

Colt stared after her as she disappeared into the fitting room. He supposed he could do anything for a few minutes. He'd consult Carolina for some kind of action plan as soon as they got home.

Later that evening Ginny found—much to her extreme consternation—that having a conversation with Brandon was indeed as tiresome as Colt had predicted. It would be fascinating to discover how his test results read, later this evening.

They'd been strolling now for nearly ten minutes, sifting through the mirky quagmire of petroleum products and their troubling political future.

There was a little piece of lint clinging to the whiskers at his chin. It was distracting and Ginny had to force herself to look everywhere but at his face. He fell silent and she frantically searched for a way to interject without looking as if she hadn't been listening.

"That's really great. I decided not to go into the family business. Luckily, I have enough brothers to pick up the slack," she offered.

"And sisters."

"Right. I have four sisters, all told."

"Is Carolina younger than you?"

"Two years, yes. Then Georgia and then Maryland and then Louise-Anna. We call her Lucy."

"Odd names."

Ginny was insulted. "They are not odd. My father is very patriotic and wanted to name all of his children after states."

"Ah. So. Ginny is short for…?"

New Jersey, you boob, she wanted to snap but didn't. "Ginny is short for Virginia."

"Ah. That's a nice name."

"Thank you." Finally she spotted Colt up ahead. "Look, Brandon! It's Colt!" She grabbed his hand and tugged him along.

"Is Carolina with him?"

"No. He's probably just passing through."

"Oh." Brandon was clearly disappointed.

Colt was mimicking the position of Rodin's famed *The Thinker* statue, when he glanced up and feigned great astonishment at their approach.

"Hello, Colt." Ginny's smile was sprightly. "What a surprise!"

"Yes. I am completely stunned, as I had no idea that you two would be passing through here this evening at this time." Colt pressed the palm of his hand over his heart. "Usually, I'm here all by myself at this time of the evening and I never expect anyone to turn up unexpectedly—"

"Of course," Ginny cut him off.

"Come here often?" Brandon asked.

Colt gave his head a grave dip. "I find it relieves the stresses of the day. I enjoy coming here and getting in touch with nature and taking time to smell the proverbial—and not so proverbial—roses.

Pressing a rose to his nose, he closed his eyes and inhaled enough pollen to choke himself half to death. Battling a coughing fit, he valiantly carried on. "But mostly I enjoy coming here to write poetry. What are you two doing here?"

"Uh…" Ginny glanced at Brandon and hoped he was buying Colt's badly acted and incredibly phony story. "We are here to, uh, to get some fresh air."

"Great idea. Nothing like fresh air. In fact, that inspires me." He paused and scribbled the words *fresh air* into his notebook. "What rhymes with *fresh?*"

Okay, where was he going with this poetry jag? *Just get to the point!* Ginny squinted at Colt, eyes blazing her message home. If he didn't cut the crap, they'd never convince Brandon to spend an evening with him this Saturday night.

"I've got the first few lines of my latest ode to Carolina nailed down, but perhaps you all could help. Okay then—" Colt cleared his throat. "'The wretched, bloody and usurping boar that spoil'd your summer fields and fruitful vines, his trough swills your warm blood like wash and makes in your embowell'd bosoms, this foul swine lies new even in the center of the isle—'" He glanced up at Brandon standing on the path and shrugged. "That's about as far as I've gotten."

"Wow. So *what else is new, Colt?*" Ginny hissed through her smile, pronouncing the *T* in his name like a firing bullet.

"Well now, let's see, what else is new?" Colt stroked his chin. "Hmm."

"Have you seen any good movies?" she prompted.

"As a matter of fact, no."

"Are you *sure?*" Her clenched jaw was beginning to ache.

"I'm sure."

"I just wondered, because Brandon, here, and I are planning to see a *movie* and wondered if you had a recommendation."

"Well now, what a coincidence! You are going to the *movies!* Now that you mention it, I do. Carolina and I are going to be taking in *Final Retribution* down at the Bijou this Saturday night—"

Final Retribution? Of all the movies in the world, he had to pick that bloodbath?

"Really? I've been wanting to see that!" she enthused and bared her teeth at Colt.

"Then you should join us!" Colt leaped to his feet. "If that wouldn't seem too forward."

"No, no…" Brandon was clearly torn between wanting to spend time with the Brubaker women and at the same time avoid Colt.

"Then it's a date, Brandon old man!" Colt grabbed Brandon's hand and gave his back a thorough slapping. "Nothing like decapitation to get the women sitting in our laps. That and some bad guys and exploding cars, well, in my book that's poetry."

Ginny yanked Brandon's hand from Colt's grip. "Okay then, *Colt.* We really should be on our way. I have dessert waiting up at the house. I'll talk to you later," she sang over her shoulder, but there was a subtle undertone that made Colt know he was in trouble.

Deep trouble.

Okay by him, he thought and, retrieving his cell phone from his shirt pocket, dialed Carolina for a report.

Over an hour had passed since Colt's meeting with Ginny in the rose garden. Since then, he'd come home to play poker on the deck with a few of the ranch hands. Kenny, Hank and the old-timers Fuzzy and Red were all seated around a picnic table munching on snacks and playing for bottle caps.

Colt glanced at his watch. He figured Ginny must have served up dessert, administered a battery of tests, compiled scores and picked out her engagement ring by now.

Time for the obligatory good-night kiss.

Colt's stomach began to churn for real.

He hated that idea. He'd hated it when she'd let Billy Payne, the chef's son, kiss her back when they were kids, and he hated it now. Although, he couldn't give Brandon a black eye, the way he had Billy Payne.

Ginny had never known about that.

But she had wondered why Billy had never come hanging around again.

Kenny won another pile of bottle caps and Colt was nearly out of the game. But try as he might, he couldn't concentrate. He knew Ginny was probably furious with him for acting like a lunatic back there in the rose garden, something about Brandon McGraw just seemed to bring out the jerk in him.

Again, he glanced at his watch.

"She's a grown-up," Kenny said.

"Who?" Colt asked, feigning innocence.

"Ginny, that's who. Dr. Ginny Brubaker, psychologist, and pretty decent judge of character."

"What makes you think I'm worried about her?"

"Because she's on a little date with McGraw and you can't seem to stop checking your watch."

"I can't stand that guy."

"Why not? He's a great guy."

"He's a great guy," Colt mimicked. "I'm sick of hearing about what a saint Brandon McGraw is. You'd think he was the Second Coming to hear the girls talk."

Fuzzy, a grizzled old bachelor, thoughtfully chewed a pretzel. "Sounds to me like you're a little bit jealous."

Colt tossed his cards to Hank. "Jealous? Me? Of what?"

Hank shuffled. "You always did have a little thingie for Ginny. I remember that, even as a little kid. You two were practically inseparable. Always burning something down or blowing something up—"

Kenny hooted. "Yeah, remember the time they slipped into a crevasse in the hay bales up in the old mow? Weren't you guys playing Luke Skywalker and Princess Leia?"

"Tarzan and Jane," Colt said with a grin. "We were swinging on that old rope-and-pulley system and ended up jammed down a crack, side by side for nearly an hour before my dad heard us screaming and came and dragged us out. Gave us both a tongue-lashing that had us both in tears."

"I could get into being stuck with her in the haymow," Fuzzy mused.

"Yup," the bashful Red agreed. "She's a looker all right."

Elbows to the table, Colt rested his eye sockets in his palms and groaned. "I blew it."

Everyone leaned forward. "Wha'd ya do?"

"I embarrassed her in front of Brandon. Again."

Fuzzy scratched his jaw. "The sooner you get over her the better. She's out of your league."

"What?" Bottle caps jumped as Colt beat his frustration on the tabletop. "This is America, man. People date whoever they want."

"Yeah, but she's a *Brubaker*. And a doctor. I hate to break it to you, but she'd be better off with someone like Brandon."

Completely honked off now, Colt upset the table as he leaped to his feet. "Why?"

"Wall…" Fuzzy drew his lips into a thoughtful, carplike frown. "I dunno, exactly. Just that's the way it's always been. The ranch hands date the town women and the Brubaker women date—"

"What Brubaker women?" Colt demanded. "All the kids who've gotten married are guys, except for Patsy. And she married a regular guy. So that shoots your theory all to hell."

"Well, danged if it don't," Fuzzy had to agree.

"Uh-oh." Red nodded at the screen door that led to the kitchen.

"What?" Colt turned around.

"The doctor is in. Mebbe we should leave y'all alone."

Colt dropped to his chair. "No! Stay here. Act natural. She won't be able to get too mad if you're all here."

Chapter Eight

The screen door slammed behind Ginny as she stormed into the cabin Colt shared with Kenny. Final retribution in her eyes, she scanned the premises, only to discover that there was a card game in full swing out on the deck. She paused, listening to the male laughter.

Drat.

She'd wanted him alone for this conversation. Looking around for a spot that might afford them some privacy, she noted that the living room, dining room and kitchen were all one open airy area. Not exactly private, but it was this, or his bedroom.

Her gaze traveled down the hall to the room with the unmade bed. She shivered. Out of the question. Keeping a clear head was a must.

Curiosity had her turning back toward the living room. It was an amazingly luxurious little cabin, doing away with the "bunkhouse" stereotype she'd drawn in her head. Orange rays of light from the setting sun streamed in from the picture window. The view was wonderful, as all the cabins were perched at the edge of a large, sparkling pond.

Inside, the furniture was rustic but beautiful. Two of the armchairs were made of smooth-hewn logs and large, overstuffed pillows covered in a hunting print and a rich brown leather couch sported colorful Indian throws. On the wall the artwork was equally engaging, and bookshelves were crowded with an assortment of classic, leather-bound books.

The place was gorgeous. Homey. Comfortable. Clean yet relaxing. And it smelled good. Manly. Like saddle soap and pipe tobacco and cedar, and Colt. Something about the personality of the room made her feel as if, for the first time in her life, she'd found home.

Her gaze shifted to the deck and stiffly her body followed. Something delicious was sizzling on the barbecue. Colt and a group of hands played cards at a picnic table that was covered by a huge umbrella. Apparently, Sunday evenings were made for relaxation and good eats.

Too bad Ginny was so far from relaxed.

As she hovered by the back door, she flexed her fists in an attempt to pull her anger under control. Colt had been deliberately boorish back there on her walk with Brandon and she wanted to get to the bottom of it.

She cleared her throat. "May I speak to you for a moment, Colt?" she called sweetly through the screen door.

Colt reluctantly stood. "Uh, sure."

He'd no sooner stepped inside than Ginny began to vent. "I thought you promised not to embarrass me out there."

"What? You said make it seem spur of the moment—"

"Yes! Spur of the moment! Not creepy!"

"And I tried not to embarrass you by stepping up to old Brandon's level with some poetry—"

"Stop calling him 'old Brandon!' And I recognized that passage from Shakespeare's *King Richard*—"

"Well, excuse me for trying to speak his language."

"Brandon does not speak Elizabethan English!"

Noting the avid interest of the guys on the deck, Colt took Ginny by the arm and led her to the living area. "Okay, maybe the poetry thing was a bit over the top."

She raked him with her narrowed gaze. "There is something about Brandon that you don't like. I can tell, I'm a professional."

"What? Brandon is a great guy. If you like that sort."

"What *sort?*"

"The portentous papa's-boy sort."

"Oh, I see what's going on here. You're jealous."

Colt froze. *She could see that?*

"Ah-ha! I'm right!"

"I—"

Building steam, Ginny rolled over his attempt at defense. "You're just angry that Brandon has money and you don't."

Colt exhaled with relief. He was jealous, all right, but not about the money.

"And you think that's why I like him. How insulting. You think I'm so shallow that I'd never marry outside my social standing. Well, let me tell you, I don't care if he didn't have a dime. I'd...I'd...like him just the way he is!" Jaws and throat working, she attempted to swallow. A pinkish tinge crawled in streaks up her neck. "If...if our test results were compatible, of course."

Colt guffawed. "Oh, come *on*. You can't even be with the guy for a simple walk through the roses without needing me to bail you out."

"Some bailing job! Brandon must think you are a complete fool!"

"Why would I give a flying buffalo chip what Brandon McGraw thinks of me? Besides, it was *your* idea to ask me to join you on your date."

Colt and Ginny ignored the four noses pressed to the deck door. A trout burst into flame on the grill.

"Yes, because I thought you'd care enough about me to help make things nice."

Pain contorted her face and Colt could only stand there in defenseless silence, bound by the pact he'd made with Carolina.

"You—" she sniffed and swiped at her eyes "—must *hate* me. What have I done to you to make you treat me so abominably?"

"Nothing! I—" Colt was at a loss. *She thought he hated her?* Good grief, the opposite was true. "I don't hate you. I hate you with Brandon. Big difference."

For a seemingly eternal moment, Ginny simply stood and stared.

As did the men on the deck. Smoke and flames belched from the barbecue unnoticed. When she finally found her voice it was low and the men had to strain to hear.

"You're bound and determined to prove that my scientific methods of courting are not going to work."

"What'd she say?" Fuzzy demanded.

"Didn't catch it," Red replied.

"Somebody ask 'em to speak up."

"Shh!" Kenny nudged the older men.

"No!" Colt denied. "It's just—"

Dropping her hands, Ginny slapped her thighs. "I don't want to hear your pathetic excuses. Right now I'm so furious at you I could smack you silly. But I won't. For Carolina's sake. For some reason, she seems to see your redeeming qualities. So, I will see you this Saturday at the movies and dinner, where I trust you will carry on a civilized conversation. Or else."

With that, she spun on her heel, marched out of the cabin and slammed the front door in his face before he could respond.

Colt balled his fists. Oh, he'd provide civilized conversation, all right. But if he and Carolina were successful, that is the only thing that would be civilized.

The very next morning Ginny was still fuming over a continental breakfast in her room. She had no intention of going downstairs to the kitchen where she knew the ranch hands gathered for coffee on Monday mornings to plan the week's work.

After much analysis, in the wee morning hours, Ginny had decided that the only smart thing for her to do was to lay low for the rest of the week. Obviously Colt had some hidden agenda when it came to sabotaging her plans to woo Brandon McGraw. Well, Ginny could spot passive aggression a mile away and she simply had no time for it.

Disappointing, though. She'd always thought of Colt as one of her staunchest supporters. And now? Now he was acting like some kind of...big brother. Good grief, she was nearly thirty. She already had three obnoxiously possessive big brothers.

What did he think he was doing?

Ginny frowned into her melon balls. He was acting out for some reason. But why? His negative attitude toward Brandon was so out of character. So completely unfounded. Why, Brandon McGraw was certainly harmless. Noncontroversial. Tame.

Beige.

Colt should be happy for her. Thrilled that his old chum was going after and getting what she needed out of life. Not thwarting her efforts.

Ginny took a deep breath and allowed her eyes to shift to the rolling lawn out the window beyond her veranda. Never mind. She was on vacation. She wasn't here to figure out what was wrong with Colt Bartlett. If he needed psychoanalysis, then it would have to be some other time.

Having made up her mind, Ginny quickly dressed for a day spent reviewing Brandon's test scores in Miss Clarise's delightful Japanese garden, where the fountains burbled one into complete tranquillity in a matter of moments.

Unfortunately, when she returned to her room late that afternoon, the rollicking party in progress put an end to her serene state of mind.

So much for laying low this evening.

For, when Ginny opened her door, there *he* was, plopped on a beanbag in her parlor, playing a rousing, thoroughly rowdy game of Monopoly with her sisters and cousins.

Here. In her room. Again.

One would think they had nowhere else to go. The Chinese take-out boxes were strewn yon and yonder and empty bottles of soda and beer and other sundry party paraphernalia littered the floor. Someone had made a run to the video store and a stack of the latest DVD releases and classic videos lay in a heap on the couch.

The smoke from five very pungent Cuban cigars filled the room and the stereo was blaring so loudly Ginny could literally see the bass vibrating the knickknacks on her shelves.

Snatching a can of air freshener from the linen closet, she shot a potpourri path to the window, where she threw open the drapes and pushed open the door to the veranda.

"Miss Clarise is going to *kill* you guys! And I'm going to help her." With a furious flourish, she snapped off the stereo.

"There you are!" Colt said when the group finally paused in play long enough to acknowledge her presence. "We were beginning to worry."

"I see that," she said, her expression droll.

"Pull up a beanbag and plant it," Colt ordered. "Big Daddy told us all to take the rest of the day off, so here we are. Carolina, honey, deal your sister some money and hand her one of those little game pieces." He beamed up at Ginny. "You can have the dog. Or the hat. Which do you want?"

"No, thank you." Stepping around the chaos, she began to tidy. "I have work to do."

Jaw tight, blood pressure high, Ginny fumed as they played, tossing dirty clothes into the hamper and stuffing paper cups into the wastebasket.

"You'll take the doggie," Colt informed her. Ignoring her ill temper, he arranged her money. He seemed not to care that she had no intention of sitting down. "Here," he told her, "I'll roll for you while you tidy up there."

"Sorry about the mess, sis," Georgia said.

"But not sorry enough to clean up, I see."

"Nope." Carolina laughed. "Not sorry enough to do that."

A sudden fight erupted over the game.

"Go to jail!" Hank shouted at Kenny.

"Make me." Kenny grabbed his brother around the waist and the two upset the bank, causing Carolina and Georgia no end of grief.

"Stop!" Carolina shouted and, attempting to separate the boys, knocked a plate of snack food off the table in the process.

Luckily, Georgia managed to snatch the game board out of harm's way until they'd finished.

Ginny took a cleansing breath and began to sort piles of shoes.

"Ginny, will you put that stuff down and come over here and play?" Colt demanded.

"I don't have time."

"What are you talking about? You have the entire summer. I thought you came here to relax. To take some time off before you settle down and begin the daily grind of being Mrs. Brandon McGraw."

"How can I relax with all this noise?" She flicked her hand toward the others, busily cheating, pilfering each other's money, moving each other's hotels around and finally outright stealing them altogether.

"It doesn't have to be silent for a person to relax."

Finally, on her way past after tossing a load of socks and shoes out into the hall, Colt snagged her arm and yanked her down onto his lap.

"Would you stop?" he growled. Tucking his chin into his chest, he peered into her face. "You do so enjoy playing the martyr."

"I beg your pardon?"

"Oh, c'mon, admit it. You do. You love it. You've always been that way. Even when we were little. We were slobs. You were an angel." He put his arm around her shoulder and pulled her close, and rolling her back on the beanbag, rubbed his knuckles across the top of her head.

Confound it!

She hated it when he was right.

And she hated how she loved lying next to him this way, with him laughing and teasing.

"I do not," she protested, simply because she had no intention of letting him have the upper hand. Or of joining in on this depraved Monopoly game, for that matter. Battling the laughter she felt rising, she tried to still his roving hands. "I do not enjoy playing the martyr."

"You do, too."

"Do not!" She willed herself not to crack, even though his fingers were probing her ribs and driving her crazy. This was no laughing matter. She may be a martyr but she certainly didn't enjoy it. Besides, she'd never agree with him. She had her pride. She wriggled and flailed but she was no match for his strength.

He dragged her across his lap and blew a raspberry on her belly, which had her howling with indignation that finally bubbled over into laughter. Nobody seemed to notice, let alone mind.

Finally they grew still, their gazes flicking from eyes to lips as they remembered the kiss they'd shared. Ginny's breathing came in shallow little puffs and she could hear her heart throbbing in her ears.

Colt bent his head, his mouth hovering over hers, and for a moment Ginny was sure he was going to kiss her, and she wanted him to. More than anything, she wanted a repeat of those glorious moments they'd shared out by the tent at the barbecue. Then she remembered where they were.

And who they were with.

She shot a glance in Carolina's direction, but her sister was so busy prying hotels out of Kenny's hands, one would be tempted to think she'd forgotten that the love of her life was even in the room.

Slowly Ginny sat up and straightened her clothing. Colt followed suit and they acted as if nothing had happened.

So, Monday night it was Monopoly and Chinese takeout and then a movie, all sitting right next to Colt. Not that she had much of a choice. All of the other chairs were taken and she was pretty well wedged in next to him on the beanbag for the duration.

No one went home until 2:00 a.m., and the infernal Monopoly game was nowhere near finished. No matter. They'd simply finish tomorrow. Here. In Ginny's room.

Ginny didn't bother protesting.

After everyone had left, there were forgotten sunglasses and candy and gum wrappers and popcorn bowls everywhere. Not to mention wet swimsuits and towels on her bed and floor. Her pillow and comforter were soaking.

For once she was too tired to obsess. Ginny wandered back to the beanbag chair she'd shared with Colt all evening. Falling into the comfortable imprint of their bodies and dragging an afghan over her shoulders, she reveled in the warmth and subtle scent of Colt.

When Tuesday night arrived, they finished the previous night's bogus Monopoly game and gobbled a load of sub sandwiches. There were bits of shredded lettuce and chip crumbs everywhere. Hank spilled his cola, turning the sandwich bags and napkins into a sticky mess.

Again, Colt insisted that Ginny stop her infernal cleaning and sit down and be sociable.

Because her feet were killing her, Ginny complied a little more readily than she had the night before. But she grumbled a bit, just so everyone would know that she did not approve of their freeloader attitude toward her room.

Since everyone was sitting in the same position required to play Monopoly, Ginny once again ended up on the beanbag next to Colt. She could feel his warmth penetrate her stiff muscles and she found herself sinking against him again. It was just like coming home.

If the house was on fire.

What on earth was wrong with her? Heaven help her, being so near him had her cheeks burning, her stomach melting and her skin tingling. Guilty pleasure filled her to the brim and then spilled over into fear. She was enjoying this just a tad too much.

Deciding she needed a bit of distance, she leaned away and battled back her inappropriate attraction by trying to affect a nonchalant pose. Now that Colt and Carolina were an item, she couldn't allow these feelings to take root.

Colt landed on her property and tossed her a sexy wink as he paid her off.

Too late.

The feelings had roots. And branches and leaves and flowers and…sap.

Oh, she was such a sap. The only thing that kept her from shouldering complete culpability was that, though Colt and Carolina called each other nauseating pet names like "puddin'-buns" and "boogie-nights" and made smoochie faces across the table, they didn't seem all that inclined to pay special attention to, or sit next to, each other.

It was an oddity that Ginny couldn't help but note, especially given that Colt was really very...appealing, and Carolina never missed the opportunity to sit next to the best-looking man in the room. Hardly the way she'd treat Colt if he were her boyfriend.

If Colt were her boyfriend, she certainly wouldn't allow him to sit next to another woman and gab all evening. Especially in a cozy beanbag chair, plastered together. Even if it was just her sister. And even if her sister and Colt had been best friends since they were knee-high to a rattlesnake.

And, for pity's sake, she'd certainly make time to have him all to herself. Good grief, how did one get any courting done in this zoo?

Colt reached across her to hand the dice to Kenny and yet another bolt of lightning flashed up her spine and thundered into her throat, threatening to reduce her into a tiny pile of ashes.

Then again, she supposed anything was possible.

Gnawing the inside of her lip, she glanced up at Colt's handsome face and felt her stomach lurch. Yes, her sister was really quite remiss here. As much as she had tried to ignore it, Colt was a very sexy man. He exuded raw power and an animal magnetism that held her rooted to his side, even though she knew staying in this spot was wrong.

Colt glanced at her and Ginny was terrified that everyone in the room could tell how she felt as she returned his knowing smile. Impulsively, he leaned forward and grazed her nose with his lips. Her eyes fell closed.

He'd kissed her nose!

What did that mean?

Turning away from him, she grabbed a roll of paper towels, tore several off and began scrubbing at a cup ring on the game table.

Ginny's heartbeat pounded in her ears as she polished the stubborn stain. "Miss Clarise should have demanded a cleaning deposit. Here. Use these." Grabbing a stack of coasters, she passed them out and with a wave of her hand demanded that everyone use theirs. She positioned her coaster next to Colt's and mopped the sweat from their cans. Then she dabbed at the sweat on her forehead.

She needed to find another place to sit without seem-ing...obvious. Carolina should be sitting here, not her. He should be kissing *Carolina's* nose and making meaningful eye contact with *Carolina*. And Carolina should be melting into a puddle of bliss. Ginny had no right to undermine that. Plus, she had her sights set on...what's-his-name.

Brandon.

Brandon. How could she forget poor Brandon? Four out of five psychiatrists surveyed knew that he was the most likely candidate. What was she think-ing, sitting here like some kind of hormone-ravaged teenybopper, salivating over Colt, when all of her fu-ture plans revolved around making the sensible choice. Brandon was for her. Not this laid-back cow-boy with a grin that could get a clock running in re-verse and a compelling gaze that could force a compass to point south.

She had to get away. Ginny clutched the coffee table

and managed to leverage herself to a standing position. From there, she catapulted to the veranda. The black iron railing was cool in her hands as she sucked in great breaths of fresh air.

"You okay?"

Colt's baritone came from directly over her shoulder. Rats. She needed space. Time to think things out. To convince herself that she was impervious to the baser instincts.

"Fine," she chirped. "Why do you ask?"

"You seem a little tense."

He moved toward her and gripped the railing. Trying to appear breezy, she took a step away.

"Tense? Really?" she affected some carefree laughter that fell flat.

"Mmm, hmm. Missing Brandon?"

"Brandon? Of course. Yes, as a matter of fact, I was just standing here thinking about that very thing."

"You were, were you?"

"With his business acumen, I'd imagine he'd make a mean Monopoly player."

"Can't feature old Brandon playing games for some reason. Guess I figure his silk tie might get in the way."

"I'm sure he knows how to have a good time."

"In the right company, probably."

Ginny frowned. What did he mean by that?

"You comin' back inside?" Colt stepped to the door.

"In a minute."

"Okay." His gaze lingered on her, seeming to reconcile the woman with the child. A tender smile graced his lips just before he moved inside.

Elbows propped on the railing, Ginny dropped her head into her hands. Why oh why did she have to choose now, of all times, to notice that Colt was some kind of Greek god? And why was it that Colt had never made it to her list? Certainly he had many of the qualities she cherished.

But then again, he was Colt. Her friend. Her confidant. Nothing had changed.

She set her jaw.

Nothing.

And that's how she would force herself to think of him now. Simply a studlier version of her good old buddy Colt. Nothing more. Nothing less.

Sublimate, she chanted under her breath and, resolve steely, marched back into the parlor and indulged in the age-old practice of denial.

By Wednesday it was a given that everyone would meet in Ginny's room. No matter. One jump ahead, Ginny had devised a plan she was sure would thwart the budding crush she was developing on Colt.

They'd play Twister. And, inspired by Colt's comments, she'd invite Brandon.

She dialed Brandon's office just before closing and waited as the phone rang.

"Hello?"

"Hello, Brandon?"

"No, this is his partner. Brandon is out of town."

"Out of town?" She hadn't expected that.

"Until Friday. Can I give you his voice mail?"

"Friday?" He could certainly have mentioned that in passing. "I— No, no thank you. No message." Slowly she hung up the phone and sank to the edge of her bed. So much for plan A. She was contemplating conjuring up an illness when the entire gang burst through the door.

Without knocking.

Ginny didn't bother putting up a pretext of annoyance, but instead resigned herself to the idea that her room was not her own. Closing her eyes, she took a deep breath and gave herself a little lecture.

You don't have to entertain these thoughts toward Colt. Just because you are a tad on the obsessive-compulsive side does not mean that you have to let thoughts of his thick, wavy hair and his midnight-black eyes and his broad, manly shoulders...

She shook her head. Blast.

It seemed that no matter what she told herself, when Colt ambled through the door, her heart raced a little faster.

Carolina flopped onto the couch and announced that she was sick of Monopoly.

"Me, too" Georgia sighed, and flopped next to Carolina.

"What's this?" Carolina held up the Twister game that Ginny had dug out of Patsy's closet.

"Oh, that." Ginny reached out to take the box. "That's just one of Patsy's old toys. Here. I'll put it away." There was no way she was going to play that game without Brandon.

But Carolina had no intention of giving up such a novel way to spend an evening. "No way! I say we play!" She opened the box and dumped the contents on the coffee table.

Ginny opened her mouth to protest but was completely ignored as her sisters and cousins began to rearrange the furniture. Before she knew what had hit her, they'd spread out the plastic mat, decided who would start and spun the spinner.

"Kenny," Carolina instructed. "Put your right foot on a yellow dot."

"Which one?"

"How should I know? Pick the prettiest one, you doof."

Kenny stared at the row of identical dots then made his choice.

"Good boy." Carolina slapped his rump then gave the spinner a vigorous spin. "Okay, Ginny, you have to put your left hand on a green dot."

"Uh, no…you know…" Ginny stretched and yawned and pointed at her bed. There was no way that she was going to play this game with Colt Bartlett. It was just a little too cozy for comfort. "I'm beat. I think I'll…just…uh, go in there and take a little nap."

Everyone stared as if she'd lost her mind.

"Are you crazy? You'll never get any sleep with us making so much noise. Come on. Just put your left hand on the green dot."

"No, really, I'd rather—"

"Put your hand on the green dot!" Seemed Carolina was tired of arguing.

Muttering under her breath, Ginny complied. This was completely against her better judgment.

"Colt, you put your right hand on a red dot, there, honey." Carolina leaped forward to guide him into position next to Ginny. "That's nice." She gave his derriere a little pat.

"With a tiny moustache she would make a regular dictator," Colt whispered to Ginny.

Ginny snickered. "Yeah, she's got a bit of a Napoleonic thing happening there."

Colt brought his face to hers and grinned. "I think the blood is rushing to my head," he whispered.

"Come to think of it, I'm feeling a little dizzy, too," she whispered, not sure if it was the position or the man.

"Georgia, right foot, blue dot. Kenny, right hand, yellow dot. Good, good." Carolina jumped up and down with glee. "Colt, red foot, right dot."

Colt frowned at Ginny. "Red foot?"

Ginny giggled. "Take my advice and just do it or she'll scream at you."

They snickered the way they used to, when they were up to no good as kids.

Right hand, left hand, right foot, left foot, dot, dot, dot.

Soon Ginny and Colt were hopelessly entangled, while everyone else seemed to be hovering around the perimeter.

Ginny could feel Colt's laughter breeze against the little hairs on the back of her neck. She could smell the fresh, clean scent that was so uniquely Colt, all she had to do was handle something that belonged to him to feel an odd yearning deep in the pit of her belly. And his voice. At the sound of his mellifluous timbre, she'd go weak in the knees.

Much the way she was now.

Unable to take the stress a moment longer, Ginny pretended to fall. "I'm out," she called, and crawling between the jungle of arms and legs, headed out of her room, into the hall, down the stairs and outside for a brisk, head-clearing jog, where Colt couldn't find her.

Back in the room, Carolina shot Colt a thumbs-up.

Thursday night after everyone had congregated at the usual place and time, Carolina announced, "I think we should make espressos and play charades tonight."

Apparently, they meant the kind of highly caffeinated charades that required the players to jump on her bed and gesticulate and gyrate and flail about in order to get the point across. And if the point was thigh-slapping, stupefying laughter, they were successful.

Friday evening was spent in the pool—blessedly giving Ginny a break from hostess duty—horsing around, followed by a make-your-own-sundae party in the kitchen.

It was during the construction of a fat-free, no-sugar-added banana split that her sister Carolina dropped a bombshell that rendered Ginny dumbstruck.

"Colt," Carolina mumbled around a mouthful of rocky road, "I think we should register for these ice-cream flutes when we get married."

Ginny's heart stalled and she stared, agog. *Married?*

Colt's head jerked up and he glanced from Ginny to Carolina and back to Ginny again. "Uh…I…uh…yeah. Ice cream is always good. I like ice cream." He lifted a *where-are-you-going-with-this?* eyebrow at Carolina.

"Married?" Ginny croaked.

"Sure." Carolina waved her spoon around. "We figure that the test results don't lie. Why waste time looking for other people when paradise is right here." Smile wide, she winked at Colt. "Right, honey?"

"Uh…paradise. Sure. Right." Colt nodded into the bottom of his dish.

"But, but," flabbergasted, Ginny stammered. "*Married? Why…married?*"

"It was your idea. Wasn't it her idea, Colt?"

"My idea?" Ginny blanched. Had she started this ball rolling? "When did I—? When were you planning to…tie the knot?"

"Probably not until, you know—" Carolina frowned off into space "—the end of summer or something. Give us time to make all the arrangements."

"This summer?" Ginny shrieked.

Hank, Kenny and Georgia looked on with interest. "You guys are getting married this summer?"

Colt glanced from sister to sister.

Shoulders bunched, Carolina said, "Sure. Why not?"

"I'll tell you why not! Because you haven't spent any time together since we were little kids. Even then, you and Colt never played together. He played with me! Me, not you!" Ginny could feel the tips of her ears catch fire.

"But we plan to rectify that, huh, Colt?"

Colt gave his head a noncommittal wobble. "Yeah?"

"Oh, come *on!* When have you had time to make such an important decision? You haven't been alone together for more than thirty seconds at a time. What are you thinking?"

Carolina's forehead puckered. "But you said that we—"

"Forget what I said! You can't make up your minds that you are going to marry on such limited criteria."

"Why not? You are."

"I'm not *rushing!* I'm giving my relationship with Brandon a chance to bloom. I'm testing the waters before I simply dive into the deep end."

"Well, we have our results, Ginny. You have convinced us that waiting for love to come a'calling is a big waste of time. We're getting hitched."

Chapter Nine

Eyebrows high, everyone exchanged glances as Ginny rushed from the room. In the ensuing moments, the once boisterous party withered and died on the vine. Silence fell, save for the ticktock of the kitchen clock, which seemed to suddenly thunder throughout the room.

"What's up with her?" Georgia finally wondered in a half whisper as she popped the lid back on the chocolate sauce.

Kenny focused on his sundae. "I think it came as a little shocker to find out that her sister and her best friend are getting married—" he angled his chin and squinted at Colt "—in such a cavalier manner."

"Really?" Georgia shrugged. "I think it's great."

Colt plunged both hands through his hair. "Oh, come on. It's not as if we're actually going to—"

"Colt," Carolina interrupted. "Colt, could I see you outside for a minute?"

"Yeah, sure, in a sec." He waved a dismissive hand at Carolina and continued in his defense to Kenny. "You know that all this stuff about me and Carolina getting marr—"

"Colt!" Carolina tugged on his sleeve.

"What?"

"I need to talk to you." An ersatz grin plastered across her face, Carolina jerked her head toward the back door. *"Now."*

The full moon shone through the trees and illuminated the gourmet herb garden near the kitchen's back door as Carolina led Colt outside. The air was warm and as still as the marble statues that graced strategic areas in this charming, fragrant wonderland. Off in the distance the crickets were in full symphony with the pond frogs.

Colt had always loved this place. It was rumored that his father had proposed to his mother—then an assistant chef—right here in this very garden, on a night not too unlike this one. It was nearly four decades ago now.

His sweet mother was gone.

His father was retired, remarried and relocated to Phoenix.

Talk about history.

Beyond the herb patch, small path lights lit a tree-lined passage to a box hedge maze situated behind the eastern wing of the main house. Clearly interested in privacy, Carolina tugged Colt down this trail and onto the brick patio at the entrance of the maze and glanced around before she gestured for him to take a seat on an iron bench near a burbling fountain.

Colt eyeballed her with censure. "Ya know, it'd be nice if you'd clue me in before you go off on one of your funky tangents." With a heavy sigh, he sank to the bench and crossed his legs at the ankles.

"Yeah, I know. Sorry about that." Settling beside him, Carolina peered up into his face. "But I feel that it's time to implement phase two."

"Phase *two?* If getting engaged is phase two, what is phase three? Our wedding? Is phase four little Colt junior? Will *that* make her jealous?" He pinched the bridge of his nose. "Where is this all gonna end, Carolina?"

"Colt, listen." Carolina slipped off her sandals and, tucking her legs beneath her, leaned toward him in excitement. "Don't you get what just happened back there? We're forcing Ginny to take a long hard look at her by-the-book, nonemotional, completely insane approach to relationships!"

"Yeah, but—"

"She's so damn smart, she can't see past her research and into her own heart."

"Yeah, but... She can't?"

"No!" Gesticulating wildly, Carolina drew pictures in the air as she spoke. "Okay, stay with me here, Colt buddy. Ginny thinks we're buying into her scientific ideas about love and life, right? And now she thinks we're following through by getting married without all the usual hearts-and-flowers courtship, right? And the reality of this...*freaks her out!*" She rocked to her knees and wriggled with excitement. "For once she's feeling with her heart and not her pie-in-the-sky head." The gleam in Carolina's eye was not simply a reflection of the moon.

"Yeah, but come on. I mean, she seems pretty upset and I thought we just wanted to make her jeal—"

"*Jealous.* Yes! Exactly right!" Bringing her nose near

his, Carolina clutched Colt's arm and whispered in a hushed tone. "She is jealous as hell, though she can't admit it because blood is thicker than water! She doesn't want to hurt me."

"But, okay, *that's* where you lose me. How is that going to make her fall into my arms?"

"She loves us *both.* She wants what's best for us *both.* Eventually she's gonna see that what's best for me is *not you.* And what's best for you is *her."*

"And the best way to that end is to let her think we are getting married?"

"No." Carolina's arms flailed. "The best way to that end is to let her think we are rushing into a loveless marriage based on carnal needs like lust and a batch of stupid test results! That's what's gonna bring her to her senses. Because she loves us, she has to save us. And by doing so—" Carolina's smile was triumphant "—she'll end up saving herself."

"You may have a point there." Colt thoughtfully stroked his lower lip. Carolina's reasoning was beginning to make some kind of kooky sense. Still, what she proposed was risky. "You don't think we're driving them closer together, do you?"

"Are you *kidding?* We need to break out the big guns if we're ever gonna make her sit up and take notice, even though the village idiot can see that she and Brandon are from different planets. We don't need a battery of psychological tests to tell us this." Carolina gave her head an emphatic shake. "No! Things are going exactly according to plan. Ginny's in love with you. Trust me. When I started talking about our marriage she turned positively green. It was a thing of beauty."

A heady feeling flirted with the corners of Colt's mouth. Ginny was jealous. How about that.

Their nutty plan was actually working.

Maybe Carolina was right. And if they redoubled their efforts, she'd be putty in his hands in no time. Inhaling deeply of the night air, he was suddenly filled with excitement. "Okay. Count me in for phase two. So, what's next?"

Carolina sprang forward and hugged him tightly around the neck. "Oh, I am so going to love having such a devious brother-in-law!" After a resounding kiss on the cheek, she sat back, her eyes aglow. "Okay, pay very close attention because this is where our plot thickens."

From her perch on the pillow-strewn window seat in her bedroom, Ginny watched Colt and Carolina as they cuddled together on a bench near the fountain. In the clear light of a moon made for romance, they sat nose to nose, lost in cozy conversation. No doubt they were discussing china patterns and picket fences and chubby babies that had their father's dark eyes and their mother's sense of fun, and a big, slobbering dog that liked to play fetch, and all manner of happily-ever-after...

Ginny pressed her fist to her mouth and blinked. Her heart was oddly leaden with feelings that in her experience signaled the onset of depression. But why? What did she have to feel bad about?

Wasn't she fulfilling all of her goals? Mapping out the perfect future? A life without the usual emotional consequences of selecting an ill-suited mate? She should be happy. Giddy. And equally thrilled for her sister and Colt. A match, by all scientific standards, made in psychological heaven.

Then why was she so miserable?

Seeds of doubt began to sprout in the back of her mind as she second-guessed her carefully educated plan. Could she be on the wrong track with her approach to finding a mate?

A heavy sigh fogged the glass as she leaned her forehead on the cool windowpane. Admitting so would discredit a great deal of her research. Years and years spent proving her theory correct.

"No," she whispered, filled with apprehension. She simply could not be wrong about this. For her, knowledge was always the preferred choice over emotion. Matters of the heart only blurred fact.

Then why wouldn't these unholy feelings for Colt go away? With every second that passed, they grew and mutated from a friendship that had made perfect sense to a mad, passionate desire that made no sense at all. She must be suffering the ravages of some kind of hormonal imbalance.

Sleep.

Yes. That was it. She was always overly emotional when she was tired. A lone tear squeezed past the eyes she'd screwed so tightly shut to block out the image of Colt with Carolina making their special plans. Until she had a good night's sleep under her belt, their happiness was more than she could bear.

Saturday morning found Ginny still battling the blues that had taken up residence in her heart the night before. Odd, considering she'd taken a sleep aid that had virtually knocked her out for a solid eight hours. She awoke well rested but miserable.

She rose, poured herself a cup of calming, decaffe-

inated herbal tea, blended to soothe the troubled heart
and quiet the anxious mind. She popped in her relaxation tape and proceeded to stretch her worries away. To
no avail.

A restlessness burned in her belly, causing her head
to buzz and her cheeks to burn. The symptoms were
nearly flulike, leaving her shaky and unable to focus.
The last time she'd felt like this, she'd been out horseback riding with Colt and Carolina.

She rummaged through the medicine cabinet and,
discovering a thermometer, took her temperature. No
fever. She opened her mouth and ahhhhh'd at the mirror. Throat looked fine and no one else in the family
seemed to be suffering.

Even so, the feeling hung on for the rest of the day,
seeming to increase in intensity whenever she thought of
Colt and Carolina getting married. Clearly her inability
to control her renegade emotions was making her sick.
She saw this type of thing in her patients all the time.

But, oh dear, her sister and Colt were making such a
huge mistake. And it was all her fault. How would she
ever be able to forgive herself if they married and it
failed?

Affirmations and positive self-talk.

That's what she needed. Gathering a pile of pillows,
she plunked into the middle of the floor, crossed her legs
and began an internal dialogue with herself.

"Colt and Carolina are a perfect, scientific match."

A stabbing pain seared her between the eyes. Ow.
She frowned and tried again.

"Brandon and I are a perfect, scientific match."

Her stomach lurched.

"Tonight's movie and dinner with Brandon will be

fun. Double dating with Colt and Carolina will certainly double the fun!" Ginny inhaled so deeply her nostrils narrowed to little slits. *"Fun, fun, funnnnnnn."* She exhaled, battling nausea and willing herself to believe. *"I believe it will be fuuuuuuunnnnnnnnnn. Ohhh, yeahhhhh, funnnnnnnnn."*

After a day spent inhaling aromatherapy candles and praying for sanity, Ginny began her preparations for an evening on the town. As she put the finishing touches on her hair, she checked her reflection in the mirror. Funny how easy it was to hide one's emotions. If she didn't know better, she'd think the woman smiling back at her was feeling in fine fettle. Enjoying the beginning phases of a relationship that might lead to her future.

As she should be.

Too bad the opposite was true.

"Funnnnnnnnnnnnnnnn," she reminded herself as she nervously smoothed the sensible outfit that Colt had helped her choose last weekend. What could be better than spending an evening in the company of the ones she loved?

As she twirled about and scrutinized the size of her rump in the mirror, Ginny was startled by a sharp rap at the door. Without waiting for her to respond, Colt and Carolina burst through and, after a breezy greeting, made themselves at home. Carolina rushed to the bathroom and pawed through Ginny's cosmetics bag for lipstick and Colt foraged in her refrigerator for anything edible. He sniffed at a stiff, half-eaten piece of pizza and, deciding it still had nutritional merit, ate it. Their clothes were nearly as loud as they were, and something about their matching outfits set Ginny's teeth on edge.

Carolina breezed out of the bathroom, blotting her lips on a tissue. "Hey, sis! You ready for an evening of *Final Retri*—"

"—*bution?*" Colt slapped Carolina's hand and they jostled each other like big, silly, frolicking—her lips pruned in distaste—otters.

So. Colt was even finishing her sentences these days. Irritation reignited Ginny's flu symptoms. She jammed her feet into her shoes and conjured up a tight smile.

"Oh, yes. Sounds like heaven."

"Then let's go pick up your man," Carolina sang, and skipped into the hall towing a hapless Colt behind her. "We don't want to keep him. I bet you guys can't wait to see each other."

"No." Ginny grabbed her small leather clutch purse and closed the door behind her. "Can't wait."

Colt drove. All the way to Brandon's, he and Carolina held hands and simpered at each other in the most nauseating baby talk. Ginny couldn't imagine Brandon ever indulging in such flights of fancy.

Then again, there were many things Ginny couldn't imagine Brandon doing.

"Honey-bunny?" Carolina cooed at Colt, her finger absently flicking his earlobe.

"Yes, lovely-dover?"

Ginny gripped her clutch and wondered how it would hold up as a barf bag.

"I've been thinking."

"Yes?"

"I don't think I want to get married next month."

Relief, like a cleansing rain, washed over Ginny. "Excellent, Carolina," she said. "I was hoping you'd come to your senses and realize it's far too soon for such a major life commit—"

"But—" Carolina twisted in her seat and shot Ginny a plaintive look "—I was going to suggest that we elope. This week. No fuss, no muss."

"No!"

"No?" Carolina glanced at Colt.

"No?" Colt arched an eyebrow and adjusted his rear-view mirror to better see Ginny.

"No, no, no, *a thousand times no!*" Ginny felt as if she might burst into flames as she threw down her clutch, gripped the backs of their seats and hauled her body between their bucket seats. "I don't want to hear another word about it until I have time to test you two again. Is that clear?"

Carolina shrugged. "You're probably right. I always wanted a big wedding anyway."

Ginny sagged back against her seat, emotionally exhausted, and the evening was only just beginning.

Oh, this was just going to be so much...*fuuuuuun.* In the Bijou's main lobby, Ginny stared at the poster for the movie they were about to see while Brandon battled the throng to order up the munchies. Colt and Carolina billed and cooed over by the water fountain.

On the poster, a man and woman squared off, guns blazing à la shootout at the OK Corral. The caption read: When a Prenup Isn't Enough...*Final Retribution.*

Ginny sighed as she thought of the counseling bill for that couple. The movie was, if not critically acclaimed, at least popular with the masses. Maybe it was better than it looked.

Arms loaded with popcorn and soft drinks, Brandon

joined her and together with Colt and Carolina they navigated their way into the darkened theater. After a lengthy stint spent stumbling about in the shadows, they finally found two pairs of empty seats in the center of the room. Ginny and Brandon took the set directly behind Colt and Carolina. Once they were settled, Ginny passed out the treats and attempted to focus on the coming attractions.

But it was impossible.

Clearly, the only attractions Colt and Carolina were interested in were each other. They fed each other popcorn and sipped each other's drinks and nuzzled, and nibbled on each other's necks in a most obnoxious manner. Worse than a couple of teenyboppers alone in a closet, they whispered and giggled and attracted dirty looks from everyone within a twenty-foot radius.

They didn't seem to notice. Or care.

Ginny squirmed in her seat. All the oxygen in the theater seemed as if it were being sucked up by the standing-room-only crowd. To her left, an old man's nose whistled as he breathed. Behind her, a teenager kicked her seat. On her right, Brandon spread out, hogging the armrest and infringing on her limited legroom with his giant feet.

In front of her, Colt and Carolina had tossed a sweater over their heads and seemed to be locked in a clinch that would result in the conception of their first child by the end of the second act. Ginny tried not to look, but like a train wreck it was impossible not to stare. They were just so…active.

Shifting position, she forced herself to concentrate on the screen.

Plastic rattled as Brandon struggled to tear open a bag

of Gummi Bears. In her peripheral vision, she could see him grinning sheepishly at her. More crinkling cellophane. More determined grunting.

Ginny gritted her teeth and grinned back.

Rattle.

Rattle, rattle, rattle.

Blessedly, Brandon's bag finally popped open. Silence reigned for a good ten seconds until he began to painstakingly extract his candy, one cursed bear at a time. As Brandon chewed, a variety of artificial-fruit aromas assailed her nostrils, and each time he swallowed he'd emit a little grunt.

The same little grunt he'd emit when something was funny. Or hysterical. Or scary. Or horrifying. Same grunt. Covered all emotions. And flavors.

And in front of her, Colt and Carolina honeymooned.

Bathed in misery, Ginny stared at the giant movie screen through blurry eyes and tried to envision sitting here, next to Brandon, until death did they part. He fumbled with a box of red vines, muttering, crinkling cellophane and mashing the box.

Impossible. That much was suddenly crystal clear. She pulled her lips between her teeth and battled the urge to tear the box from his hand and hurl it across the room.

To hell with his test scores.

This man drove her half out of her tree. She hated his stupid grunts. The way he endlessly chewed his popcorn and noisily slurped the last bit of soda from the bottom of his cup. She detested the way he sprawled out, forcing her into the whistler on her left.

Nothing about Brandon attracted her physically, from his too-perfect teeth to his too-styled hair. Oh, he was nice enough looking and all that, but he simply didn't compel her.

Not the way Colt did with a single glance. He didn't smile like Colt, he didn't laugh like Colt, he didn't tease like Colt, he didn't care about her like Colt, and to top it off, he didn't even smell like Colt.

Feeling as if he was about to suffocate, Colt pushed the sweater off his and Carolina's heads, causing their hair to stand on end from the static electricity.

"She'd sure as hell better be looking because I'm sweating like a pig here," Colt griped.

Carolina peeked through the sweater's loose weave. "Oh, yeah. She's watching. And she looks mad."

"Well, no wonder. Between our Olympics and Brandon's endless, torturous paper rattling—"

"What rattling?" Carolina whispered, her face puzzled in the flicker of the screen lights. "I didn't hear anything."

"You can't be serious. You mean to tell me that you haven't noticed that it takes Brandon at least twenty minutes to open one idiotic bag of candy?"

Carolina shrugged. "No?"

"Then I suppose you haven't noticed the geezer behind me that whistles when he breathes, either?"

"Nuh-uh."

Colt rolled his eyes. "Are you deaf, woman?"

"No, but I am starving. When's this flick over?"

"Not soon enough." Colt dragged the sweater back over their heads. "Not soon enough.

At the restaurant, things went from bad to worse.

Carolina and Colt laid it on so thick over dinner, Ginny feared they'd tip the table over. All the while,

Brandon continued to find little ways to irritate her. When he wasn't shredding his drink doily, or noisily chasing and scraping the last grain of rice from his plate, he prattled endlessly about gas. *Gas, gas, gas.*

What on earth was so blasted interesting about gas?

Taking a deep, somewhat unladylike slug of her wine, Ginny sat back and reviewed a few simple affirmations. *She and Brandon were a perfect, scientific match.*

Oh, yeah.

She drained her glass.

After a few minutes she was feeling a tad more charitable and told herself that she really wasn't trying very hard. Certainly not as hard as Colt and Carolina had been trying. Just look at them. Now *there* was some serious trying. They'd taken their test results and run.

Okay. What was wrong with her? After all, this whole mess had been her idea. And yet she seemed to be the only one wallowing in misery. So, after refilling her glass, she made an attempt not only to put up with Brandon's idiosyncrasies, but to find them endearing. Any man who enjoyed Gummi Bears couldn't be all bad. In future, she'd simply offer her purse clippers and help him with the bag.

She focused on Brandon's perfect teeth and wondered if they were really his. When he came to a spot in his gas diatribe where she could inject a little levity, she threw back her head and emitted some tinkling laughter. And when he slurped at his drink, she tossed back a gulp or two of her own. And when he practically scraped the pattern off the china in pursuit of the last crumb of his dessert…Ginny polished off her second glass of wine.

And…Brandon old boy was even beginning to look

ever so slightly appealing. In a gassilicious sort of way. Ginny giggled and burped into her napkin.

Colt didn't get it. If Ginny was so much in love with him, why was she falling all over herself to get Brandon-the-crashing-bore's attention? The way she was fawning and giggling and laughing over the latest Petroleum Institute policy issues, he'd be tempted to think she was seriously enjoying herself.

Had he and Carolina gone too far, back there at dinner? he wondered as he nosed his rig out of the parking lot and into traffic. Had she finally given up on him?

From the shadows of the back seat, Brandon nattered on about his petroleum stock holdings. What either of the Brubaker women saw in him was beyond Colt. Certainly it wasn't his money, as the Brubaker family was loaded, so what was it? Colt rotated his head to relieve some tension. Maybe Brandon exuded some of those powerful sex pheromones that made women go deaf and blind to his peculiarities. He shrugged. Being that he wasn't a woman, the attraction eluded him.

In less than an hour Colt pulled up in front of Brandon's impressive house and cut the engine. After some stilted good-night pleasantries, Ginny stepped out and walked Brandon to his front door. The porch light was blazing. Colt and Carolina were riveted by the drama that unfolded.

"Think he'll kiss her good-night?" Carolina whispered.

"Think he can stop talking about gas long enough?"

"That's not nice. I wonder what kind of kisser he is."

Colt shrugged. "He's great. I really enjoyed our last kiss but that's just me."

Carolina slugged him and giggled nervously. "Very funny."

They hunched toward the windshield to see better but only ended up fogging the glass. Colt turned the defroster on full blast and they both swiped at the condensation with their sleeves.

"What are they doing?"

"Nothing. Yet."

They held their breath as Ginny leaned in for the obligatory good-night kiss. Brandon followed suit, and gripping her upper arms, held her just close enough to give her a quick and chaste peck on the cheek. Both Colt and Carolina sighed their relief, fogging the window again. They hurriedly polished view holes and watched as Ginny and Brandon awkwardly bid each other good-night.

"That was horrible." Carolina grinned.

"Mmm." Colt nodded. "The man's a wimp."

"He is not! He just needs the right woman."

"Here she comes. Act natural."

"What should I talk about?"

"Anything but gas."

When they arrived back at the Circle BO, Colt parked and escorted both women to the servants' entrance.

"Thanks for a wonderful evening, Colt darlin'," Carolina said breezily.

"No, thank *you*, Carolina honey. Come here and give me some sugar."

They slurped and smacked and rocked back and forth, blocking the doorway and making it impossible for Ginny to pass. She rolled her eyes.

"Colt darlin', would you like a little coffee with all that sugar?" Carolina snapped on the kitchen lights and led the way inside. "I'll make decaf."

"Sounds good. But only if Ginny will join us."

Ginny paused at the refrigerator to grab a glass of ice water so that she could take her daily vitamins. "Whatever," she groused. She might as well stay up as she sure as heck wasn't going to get any sleep tonight. A search of her tidy purse yielded the pouch that contained her multivitamins and herbal extracts. She decided to take several ibuprofen along with her B12. Her head was killing her.

Disgruntled, she choked down the pills. Why didn't Brandon kiss her the way Colt kissed Carolina?

Why didn't she want Brandon to kiss her that way?

Why *did* she want Colt to kiss her that way?

"The coffee's perking. You two help yourselves." Carolina set out two mugs and some vanilla creamer.

"Where are you going?" Ginny demanded.

"I have a phone call to make."

"At this hour?"

"Is it late?" Carolina asked over her shoulder as she floated out of the room.

The aroma of fresh-perked java filled the air and Colt filled their mugs.

"Cream?"

"Whatever," Ginny snapped.

"Feeling out of sorts?"

"Buzz off."

Carrying the mugs to the granite-topped island, Colt took a seat next to Ginny.

"What's the problem?"

"What makes you think I have a problem?"

"I don't know. Perhaps it's your cheery disposition."

"It's late, okay?"

"You wanna know what I think?"

"No."

"I think you're just mad because you didn't get to make out at the movies like me and my sugar-booger."

"I am not," Ginny argued hotly. "And don't call her that. It triggers my gag reflex."

"Plus, I really don't believe you enjoyed your goodnight kiss from Brandon."

"Did too."

He laughed.

Ginny glared at him. "Besides. How would you know if Brandon was kissing me back in the theater? Your face was stuck to Carolina's!"

"I know he wasn't kissing you because he was busy cramming his face with Gummi Bears!

"He was simply enjoying his snacks."

Noses together, they began to bicker as they had when they were kids.

"And so was I!"

"That may be so, but clearly Carolina's charms did not captivate you enough to render you oblivious to what was going on behind you!"

"I can see you're going to be grumpy until you get kissed properly. I'll call Brandon."

"Blow it out your ear." Ginny stood and marched her mug over to the sink.

Colt followed with his. "Just admit it. Brandon is a wimp."

"No!" Ginny spun to face him, her cheeks blazing, her lungs laboring. "He's not a wimp. Just because he didn't try to take advantage of me in the theater is no—"

Colt stepped forward and slipped his arms around her waist.

Suspicious, Ginny squinted up at him. "What are you doing?"

He backed her against the countertop and sank into her. Automatically, she slipped her arms around him for balance and ran her hands over the muscular planes of his back.

"I'm gonna give you that kiss good-night."

Ginny swallowed a little gasp. "And…and…what if I don't want a kiss good-night?"

A low chuckle rumbled in his chest. "Then I'll know."

"How?"

With one hand he cupped the back of her head and angled it so that he could look directly into her eyes. "First I'll kiss you just once, like this." He bent forward and allowed his lips the briefest of contact, and pulling back, let them hover over hers.

"Ohh." She could feel her sigh rebound off his lips.

"And then, if you arch into me—just the way you are now—with your mouth half-open and your eyes half-closed, I'll know I can…do…this."

Colt dipped his head again for a kiss that was even more exquisitely tender and talented than the one they'd shared the night of Big Daddy's barbecue.

And Ginny was lost.

All rational thought escaped her, and for the first time in her life she didn't care. Greedily, she clung to him, standing on tiptoe to better offer her mouth.

He braced one arm on the countertop and took her up on her offer. For the longest time they stood, voraciously consuming each other, lavishing, luxuriating in each other's kiss. Their breathing was ragged, their hearts were pounding, their hands moving.

Colt pulled back just long enough to sigh into her mouth. "Oh, Ginny." And he kissed her again.

He kissed her hard and long and deeply enough to

span the years. To make up for not being her first, for Billy Payne's inept attempt, and most especially, for her misguided beliefs that science was better than this.

Ginny groaned. How could she have been so foolish? This was heaven. Dreamily, she pressed ever closer, reveling in his mouth's explorations of her cheeks, lips, eyelids. Delicious sensations assailed her from the top of her head and down her spine to the tips of her toes.

She simply could not fathom doing this with Brandon. Simple things like gasping his name, threading her hands through his hair, admiring the bulk of his bicep with her fingertips would be physically impossible. And no matter how they might score on paper, in the flesh it couldn't happen.

Colt, oh, Colt.

Why didn't she see it all sooner? Her lips traveled the stubble on his jaw and she nuzzled his neck with her nose. He'd always been right there, and she too smart to see it.

Suddenly Colt set her upright from where he'd had her bent over the countertop and—after kissing her one last, lingering time—took a shaky step back and raked a palm over his face.

"That's how he ought to be kissing you by now."

And with that rather blunt announcement, Colt stalked out of the kitchen.

From outside, the sound of his engine roaring to life was his only goodbye.

Chapter Ten

Stunned, Ginny touched her lips and watched Colt's headlights fade into the distance.

She'd just kissed her sister's sweetheart.

Guilt, like the bowels of a volcano, suddenly flared in her gut. She bit back a remorseful sob. Poor Carolina. She would be so hurt if she knew. Slowly, Ginny climbed the back servants' steps that led to her second-floor suite. What on earth was the connection she shared with Colt that could allow her to betray her own flesh and blood with such wanton abandon?

For what seemed an aeon, she paced back and forth in front of her window and wrestled with the hows and whys. How would she ever face Carolina again? Her dear little sister.

Slowly, her fear gave way to anger. What right did Colt have, playing with her emotions this way?

She glanced at the clock. Nearly midnight. Tough.

Acting on impulse for once in her life, she picked up the phone and dialed his number.

"Hullo?" came the sleepy answer after two rings.

"How dare you toy with my emotions this way?" By this time, she'd reached a slow boil.

"Huh?"

She grimaced. "Oh. Hi, Kenny. Is Colt there?"

"Uh…" Kenny let loose with a loud, howling yawn. "Lemme go see. I was just lying here…sleeping and uh…"

He didn't bother to cover the receiver as he shouted. *"Colt? Hey, Colt?"*

"Yeah?" came a muffled reply from another room.

"You're wanted on the phone." Kenny came back on the line. "G'night, Ginny."

"'Night, Kenny."

It seemed like forever before Colt picked up the phone in the kitchen. "Yeh-lo."

Kenny hung up.

Now, of course, she'd lost some of her precious steam. Valiantly she tried to regroup. "I don't know what kind of joke you are playing, but that was not funny. It was…it was…rude and unfair."

"I know," Colt said, taking a bit of the wind out of her sails. "And I'm sorry."

He was? Oh. Sorry about what? That he had kissed her, or that he'd been rude and unfair? Her head spun and her heart reeled. She wanted him to be sorry about the latter. Her emotions were mixed regarding the former.

"I feel like you are mocking my research," she hurled, just because she was still contemplating the confusing nuances of his apology.

"I know. And I'm really, really sorry."

She really didn't expect this reaction. Where was her sparring partner of old? "You took advantage."

"I agree. I never should have done that to you. Please forgive me."

"Well, what about my sister?"

"I called Carolina and told her everything already."

"You...*did?*"

"Yes."

"Wha...what'd she say?"

"She understood completely."

"She...*did?* That was sure big of her."

"Yes. She knows that we are friends. And that I was trying to prove a point."

"Well—" Ginny cleared her throat "—Carolina is far more self-actualized than I'd have thought."

"She really is a wonderful girl."

"Yes. Well. Okay. I just wanted to clear the air."

"Consider it clear. Friends?"

"Sure. I...guess."

"That's what you want. Us to be friends. Right?"

Ginny gnawed at a nail. "Right."

"It's what *you* want."

"It's the way it has to be."

"Because of Brandon."

No, she wanted to scream. *No, no, no. I don't know what I think anymore. I only know it's wrong to love you.* "Because of Carolina," she whispered.

Colt sighed. "You know, I could break up with her..."

Ginny gasped. Then, as she realized he was kidding, emitted some nervous, guttural laughter. "I could never forgive myself for urging you to do something so selfish."

"But..." Colt fell silent.

Ginny clutched the phone, willing him to act selfishly for once in his life.

The silence lingered between them.

Of course. Colt was a gentleman through and through. He'd never hurt her sister that way.

"Thank you for listening to me," she whispered, tears filling her eyes and burning down her throat. "Good night."

Another long silence on his end, then he whispered, "G'night."

Ginny kicked off her shoes, tore off her clothes and tossed them in a heap on the floor. Not bothering, or caring, to carefully cleanse her face and moisturize her body, let alone brush and floss her teeth, she threw herself onto the bed and let the tears flow. How utterly horrible.

She was in love.

Deeply, truly, madly.

In love.

The feelings she bore for Colt had absolutely nothing to do with science or test results. These feelings were born of a shared history, sure, but now, more than ever, they were born of an attraction. Mental, spiritual, physical and, most of all, emotional.

Clutching the comforter, she rubbed her runny nose and groaned. What on earth was she going to do now? This was simply not in the textbook plan she'd so carefully outlined for her life. She studied psychology to *avoid* all of this emotional folderol. And now look at her.

She pulled a pillow over her face so that no one could hear her wail.

Colt sank onto a kitchen stool and dialed Carolina's cell. As he waited for her to pick up, he yanked four scalding pieces of toast from the toaster and tossed them on a plate.

"This is getting out of hand," he blurted as Carolina answered. He dug the peanut butter out of the small pantry. "I think we were too convincing back there at the movies."

The static wind of her sigh filled his ear. "Yeah. I know. I'm having the same misgivings. I mean, Brandon really seems to enjoy talking to her—"

Colt snorted. Yeah, if endless, mind-numbing national energy strategy could be construed as enjoyable.

"—and they are both so…I don't know, so button-down, you know? It really seems that they do have a lot in common, and she seems so serious about all of that test score junk, and I guess their scores were like amazingly compatible and stuff." Again, a long, static-filled sigh filled his ear. "Anyway, I just don't know what we should do next."

"Oh, great. I was hoping you'd know."

"Well, we can't really do anything tonight. I mean, it's after midnight. I don't think we should really say anything until, you know, tomorrow or something."

"No!" Colt slammed the peanut butter jar down on the countertop. "I don't want to keep the truth from her for another second. I'm going so crazy here, and I don't think even Dr. Ginny will be able to cure me." He twisted off the lid, grabbed a knife and smeared his toast with a healthy coat of peanut butter.

"But this little plan is all we've got."

"Yeah, well, it ain't working, sis. We gotta think up plan B. And soon. I'm beginning to feel like a real heel."

"Because you kissed her? Big deal. You said you were sorry. Didn't you?"

"Yeah, but I'm afraid it will happen again. Tonight!" He took a healthy bite of toast and held his thumb and forefinger up to the phone. "I'm about *this* far from scaling the trellis to her room and busting through her doors and blurting out the truth and then kissing her senseless." He paused to toss back a slug of milk straight from the carton and wiped his mouth on his sleeve. "And if I do, and she thinks you and I are still together, she'll never forgive me."

"Okay, okay. I'm putting my shoes on right now. Meet me at the pool in fifteen minutes and we'll discuss phase three or plan B or some dumb thing." Carolina yawned.

Unable to sleep after her conversation with Colt, Ginny grabbed her swimsuit and a towel and, stepping over the earlier mess she'd made on the floor, headed to the pool house in her jammies. Perhaps she could bubble her troubles away in the hot tub. It'd take some pretty big bubbles, but it was worth the chance.

After she'd changed, Ginny eased her weary body into the hot water, forgoing the jets until her body grew accustomed to the temperature. The marble seat seemed to be carved with her body in mind, and she tried to let go of the emotional stress she carried.

To no avail.

Her brain was plagued with thoughts of Colt and Carolina and Brandon and the mess she'd made by forcing everyone into specific psychological molds that clearly didn't fit anybody.

She groaned.

An owl in a nearby tree hooted at her.

"Yeah," she whispered, "if you're so smart, why

didn't you warn me about getting too big for my britches?"

The owl fell silent.

Okay. Time for a review of the facts. Facts always made Ginny feel better. Holding her hand out of the water, she began to tick them off one by one.

Carolina was in love with Colt.

Colt was in love with Carolina.

Ginny was in love with Colt.

She grimaced and shook her head.

She closed her eyes and visions of Colt holding her filled her mind.

And…as she soaked and reflected upon what had transpired between them, it suddenly occurred to Ginny that if Colt were truly in love with Carolina, he just…might…not…have kissed her *that* way.

Would he?

Her heart leaped, whether from fear or excitement she couldn't be sure. Ginny only knew she had to talk to Colt. Face to face.

Now.

Hurriedly she climbed out of the hot tub, wrapped herself in a huge, thirsty beach towel and rushed to the pool house to change into some street clothes she had stowed in there.

Inside the pool house, Ginny went still as she buttoned her blouse. She heard a truck pull up and the murmur of voices filtered in through the louvered doors to her dressing room. Why on earth would someone be coming out for a swim at this time of night? Stealthily she moved to the door and pressed her ear to the slats. *Carolina?* She frowned. And *Colt?*

Yes.

Oh…no.

Her heart thrummed so loudly she had to hold her breath to make out what they were saying. Whatever it was, it was pretty serious from the sound of things. Bathed in a cool sweat, Ginny leaned against the door frame for balance. It seemed Carolina was not her usual jolly self. Was it because of the kiss Ginny had shared with Colt?

Even though she pretended to be otherwise, Carolina had to be devastated.

Oh no, oh no, oh no. What had she done? Ginny sank to her knees, riveted by the sound of their voices, too sick and scared to move or speak.

"It's more complicated than that. I know," Colt murmured.

"Oh, Colt, I'm so in love."

"I know. Me, too"

They…were…in love.

Paralyzed, Ginny's dull gaze focused up through the slats as Colt took a seat next to her sister and drew her into his embrace.

Their murmurs grew more muffled as Carolina buried her face into the folds of his shirt.

"I know, sweetheart. And I'm so sorry about all of this. I wish none of it had ever happened."

"Oh, Colt, me, too I'm just sick. It's all I have been able to think of."

"I'm sorry."

"No. Don't. You know, ever since I was a little girl, all I've ever wanted was a marriage and children."

Colt stroked her hair. "I know. That's exactly what I want. I don't know when this yen for a family actually began in me, but I have a feeling it coincided with you, and your sisters' arrival this summer." He chuckled.

"That's so sweet."

Too numb to move, Ginny could only stare as they embraced. Tears filled her eyes and spilled over her cheeks, and the pain in her chest almost had her wondering if she was suffering from cardiac infarction. Nah. She swiped a tear.

So. Carolina had found true love. How could Ginny jeopardize that? On the other hand, how could she ever be able to face having Colt as her sister's husband? Especially knowing that she was the one who'd pushed them together. She hiccuped. Oh, what a wretch.

What a wretched, wretched...wretch.

Ginny knew how it would scar her sister psychologically if she ever confided her feelings for Colt. Not only that, but there was the permanent damage those untamed feelings could do to the family's happy dynamic.

Heavy sobs wracked her body and caused her head to throb. Blindly she crawled out of the dressing room and, dragging her towel and purse behind her, decided she could not go home. How would she face Carolina?

No. No, no. As she crawled across the floor, her tears fell and created a soggy trail of sorrow. She would go over to Brandon's house. In spite of the late hour. She paused in the middle of the floor and blew her nose on her beach towel, then scrubbed at the mascara that was surely flowing from her eyes.

What did it really matter what time it was if she was going to propose marriage? Because that was her only recourse.

For the love of crying in the night almighty, she was almost thirty. And she wanted a bunch of children. What the hell choice did she have but to try to convince Brandon to elope? It was a long shot, sure, but you don't ask, you don't get, she figured.

Mrs. Brandon McGraw.

Sorrow gripped her body, pitching her about.

Oh, Colt. Oh, Colt. Oh, Colt, how I love you.

Someday she would write the song.

But I can't love you. I have to marry another man, she hummed through her tears. *I have to marry what's-his-name.* Surely—she endeavored to give herself a pep talk as she made it to the side door of the pool house and then stumbled through the rock garden and to the servants' entrance at the kitchen—she would learn to love good old what's-his-face.

"And he, me," she babbled to herself as she slowly slogged up the stairs to her room. At the landing, she dropped her face into her hands and cried for a while until she found the energy to make it the rest of the way to her room.

When Colt married Carolina, she would be able to go to their wedding and wish them well without a single pang because she would be so very, very happily married to Brandon. Oh, so very, very happy. So much so that she would be able to overlook the whole Gummi Bear thing, and maybe even come to cherish that about him and even enjoy Gummi Bears herself. She would begin looking for recipes first thing in the morning.

She hiccuped again and swiped at her tears with her towel as she barreled into her suite. Staggering into the closet, she tore through her belongings for a suitcase, yanked it open and tossed in her clothing and shoes, higgledy-piggledy. When she'd crammed in most everything she could think of, she scrawled a message on a bit of toilet paper and taped it to her door with a plastic hair-removal strip.

After talking it through several times, Colt and Carolina finally agreed that the ruse was no longer working and it was finally time to come clean to the appropriate parties. Starting with Ginny, who was no doubt lying in bed obsessing.

Colt reached into his shirt pocket for his cell phone and dialed Ginny's number. When she didn't pick up, he dialed Georgia.

"Huh...lo?" Georgia grunted.

"Georgia, hi, it's me, Colt."

"Colt, do you have any idea what time it is?"

"Uh, late, I know. Sorry. Anyway, listen, Ginny is not answering her phone and I was wondering if you could go knock on her door."

"Now? You want me to go knock on Ginny Brubaker's door right now, at two in the morning? While she is in the middle of recharging her batteries? Are you insane?"

"Yes, as a matter of fact. Please? It's a bit of an emergency."

"Well, okay." Grumbling all the while, Georgia set down the phone and was gone for what seemed an eternity before she returned. "She's gone."

"Gone?"

"Gone."

"What do you mean, *gone?*"

"Well, according to this little note on this chunk of toilet paper, she has gone over to Brandon's place, apparently, to elope."

"What?"

"Hey. Don't yell at me. I'm just the messenger."

Colt hung up and grabbed Carolina.

"Plans A and B have backfired. We're going for plan C."

"What's plan C?"

"We'll come up with that on the way to Brandon's place."

Kenny was not happy to be playing chauffeur, especially at this hour of the morning. As he, Colt and Carolina all piled into his Land Rover, a rooster over near the henhouse cockadoodled in the dawn of a new day.

"Sorry, man," Colt lamented as he leaned into the front seat and peered at Kenny. "Couldn't be helped. My battery died."

"Well, next time turn off the stupid lights. And radio. And air conditioner..." Kenny blinked at the road as it soared under the car.

"Yeah, yeah. Can't you make this heap travel any faster?"

"Well, yes. Actually, I can make it fly at up to about a warp five, but I figured you'd want us all to get there in one piece."

Nervously, Colt beat a tattoo on Kenny's headrest. "Do you think they're still there? Do you think they're married by now?"

"Colt?" Carolina's voice quavered from the seat beside him, where she was being held back by the g-forces.

"Yeah?"

"Could you please stop talking?"

Luckily, Kenny had gone to school with the guard at the gate to Brandon's house and he allowed them to hurl up the winding lane.

When the butler answered the door, it was almost as if he'd been expecting them. "Master Brandon and Dr. Brubaker have headed to a small airport just outside of Hidden Valley to board his private jet."

Colt clutched Carolina and held her upright.

"Did they say where they were going?"

"I believe—" the butler cleared his voice in a most censorious manner "—Las Vegas was mentioned as a possible destination."

Kenny gunned the engine and began to roll as Colt and Carolina leaped into the back seat on the fly.

"Where to?"

"Airport!" they shouted.

Kenny drove hell-bent for leather to the Hidden Valley airport, and they could see the blue lights of the runway within minutes.

"I wonder if they have already taken off." Carolina's lips quivered at the thought.

"Then we'll follow them to Las Vegas."

Carolina stared at Colt. "Oh, right. And how on earth are we going to find them once we're in Las Vegas?"

"We'll start going to all of the wedding chapels until we find them. And when the preacher, or judge, or whoever gets to the part where they say, 'Does anyone here know why this man and this woman can not be joined in holy wedlock?' Well, that's when you and I speak up."

"Okay."

Kenny snorted. "That's the stupidest plan I've ever heard. You guys *are* in love."

Skidding through the four-way stop and into the Hidden Valley airport's main entrance, he barreled through roads paralleling the deserted runway until he reached the hangar area where local private jets were stored. Clouds were beginning to rumble across the plains, obliterating the stars and shadowing the moon. The air took on a definite chill and mist swirled in the mercury vapor lamps that buzzed overhead.

"There they are!" Colt reached into the front seat and pointed through the fog to a clear patch under a light.

"Where?" Kenny strained unsuccessfully to see.

"There, see them?"

"No."

"Yes," Carolina screamed, *"I see them! Stop the car!"*

Shrugging, Kenny slammed on the breaks and aimed for a slot in a temporary parking area, just outside one of a dozen identical hangars.

"Ginny!" Colt shouted as he jumped out of Kenny's still-moving rig at a dead run. *"Ginny!"*

Confused, Ginny glanced at Brandon who'd been giving her an exterior tour of his jet. She held her hand up over her eyes and squinted through the swirling mist toward the tiny figure that was pounding toward her in the distance. "Colt?" she called, her eyes searching. "Is that you?"

"Ginny!"

"Colt?" Her heart leaped into her throat. The mist obscured her view for a moment.

The pounding of footsteps grew ever closer. "Gin…*neee!"*

Yes. It was Colt. Somewhere out there, stumbling around in the fog. "Colt, what in heaven's name are you doing here at this time of night?"

Kenny and Carolina were hot on his heels as Colt breathlessly emerged from the churning vapor and rushed to her side.

"I came here…" he puffed, and held up a forefinger to stall. Hands to knees, he bent over and sucked in some much-needed oxygen, "To tell you…that…" Slowly, he straightened and looking her in the eye, paused, then, "that…I love you."

Ginny's jaw dropped. "Come again?"

"I—love—you."

Minibolts of lightning cracked and thundered down Ginny's spine. Was she hallucinating? For it sounded as if Colt had just told her that he loved her. In front of Brandon and Carolina no less. Her hands cradled her throat as she ventured a glance back at Brandon and then at Carolina. She marveled over the fact that they were both smiling. Broadly. At each other.

She swallowed and swung back to face Colt. "You love me?"

"Yes." Colt took a step that brought him to her side and, dipping his head, brought his nose to hers. "And this is where you're supposed to say you love me, too"

"But…I…but…heard you and Carolina tonight, out at the pool house, making plans to marry…"

"Yes. To marry you." Colt reached for her hand and nodded at Brandon and Carolina. "And she's in love with him."

A wonder-filled smile graced Brandon's mouth as he crossed the gap between himself and Carolina and pulled her into his arms.

After a clearing shake of his head, Kenny groaned and headed back to his rig for some sleep.

Without a backward glance, Colt twined his fingers with Ginny's and began to walk. The others soon disappeared into the shadows behind them, forgotten. When they were alone, Colt drew her under the eve of an empty hangar and tipped her chin, forcing her eyes to meet his.

"I love you, Ginny Brubaker. I always have. Ever since I can remember, I've carried special feelings for you in my heart, but I don't think they really began to flower until you announced that Billy Payne had given you your first kiss and robbed me of that privilege."

"So long ago?" Ginny swallowed. "You're kidding."

"No. I'm not. And I want you to listen, and listen good. For days now, your sister and I have been trying to make you and Brandon jealous by pretending to go along with your little scientific matchmaking scheme."

"You *have?*"

"Yes, but with little effect, it seems. For some reason, you've ignored our best-laid plans, and even managed to convince yourself that Carolina and I are—" he winced "—perfect for each other."

"And you're not?"

"Oh, for Pete's sake, woman, no!"

A small bubble of relieved laughter squeaked past her lips. "You know, I couldn't believe it at first, either."

"Then why did you push it?"

Ginny sighed a puff of mist. "Because I wanted only the best for both of you. And my hypothesis…" Her shoulders flagged and she mused alone, "I think I need to rework some of my findings."

"Good." Having gained that admission, Colt rocked back on his heels and drove his point home. "And while you're at it, rework your engagement to McGraw. Ginny, Brandon is a great guy and everything, but he is all wrong for you. There is only one man who is perfect for you and I don't give a damn what the test scores say, that man is me."

Ginny's eyes snapped to his and a smile bloomed across her face. "Okay then."

"End of argument. I don't care what your stupid tests say. I love you, and I want you to be my wife and leave all your misguided expectations behind and come and live with me on my dude ranch and have us some kids."

"Okay then."

"I don't care if you want to work because, for the most part, I totally respect what you do, except for the matchmaking part. But anyway, as far as sponging off your rich family goes, I want us to make our own life. By ourselves."

"Okay then."

"Ginny, girl, I know you far too well to think that Brandon and his hoity-toity life would make you happy. You don't need a bunch of social complications to make you happy. You need simplicity. And I'm—" Colt grinned "—just the simpleton for you."

"Okay." Ginny returned his grin.

"Then—" Colt drew her into his arms and kissed her lightly on the lips "—you'll marry me?"

"Yes."

Elated, Colt held her at arm's length and peered into her eyes. "Really?"

"Really." Ginny slipped her arms around his waist and drew him close. "Because I love you, too, Colter Bartlett."

Exhaling the deep breath he'd held, Colt sagged against the door frame of the cavernous hangar and drew Ginny into his arms for a kiss meant to reassure them both that this was real and not just some dream.

"Mmm," she murmured against his lips. "I love you.

I always have. I always will." She pulled back and smiled up at him. "No simple inkblot can change destiny, I'm finally beginning to realize."

Colt's head dropped back against the building and he exhaled with relief at the stars that twinkled through the patches of cloud. "Are you sorry to have your hypothesis proved wrong?" he asked, planting light kisses upon her lips between each word.

"Are you kidding?" she sighed as he nuzzled her neck and sent a wave of gooseflesh flashing over the surface of her limbs. "I don't think I've ever been happier to be wrong in my life."

Her toes curled in her shoes as Colt cupped her face in his hands and kissed her mouth. If this was what swallowing one's pride and admitting error was all about, then bring it on, she thought muzzily.

They stood like that, simply holding each other and whispering of their love and plans of the future until the light on the horizon began to change.

"And you'll be happy living with me on a dude ranch?" Colt whispered.

"If you're there, yes."

"What about your work?"

"I'm sure there are people with problems in this neck of the woods."

"I love you," he whispered, his eyes flashing.

"I love you, too," she whispered back.

"Marry me now."

"Now?"

"Yeah. I bet we could talk Brandon into flying us to Vegas."

"Sure." Ginny laughed. "Especially if I don't make him marry me."

"Tell me that you guys weren't really running off to elope tonight."

"No. I was hurt and looking for an escape. Watching you and Carolina together…" She sighed. "But I knew deep in my heart it would never work with Brandon. And tonight, when he came to the door in his monogrammed, satin dressing robe and matching lounge slippers, it simply drove the point home."

Colt chuckled.

"When I got over to his house, Brandon was still up because he'd just closed a deal on a new jet and wanted to show it off. And since I just happened to be there…here we are. He was thinking about taking it for a shakedown cruise to Vegas and wanted to know if I wanted to go along for the ride. Until now I didn't have anything better to do…. We could be there by morning. Carolina could be my maid of honor. Kenny could be the best man."

"I like the way you think. Most of the time," he teased. Behind them, the jet's engines roared to life as Brandon showed off his new toy to Carolina.

Kenny rolled out of the back of his Land Rover and stretched and rubbed the sleep from his eyes.

Colt offered Ginny his arm. "Should we go?"

"Oh, yes." She slipped her hand into the crook of his elbow and they began to rush toward the jet.

"C'mon, Kenny," Colt shouted. "We're going to Vegas."

Kenny shrugged. "Sounds good." Shooting the locks to his rig with the remote, he ambled toward the plane.

"By the way." Ginny paused just before they embarked. "It worked."

"What worked?"

"Your little scheme with Carolina. I was jealous."

"Ah. So you *were* jealous. Don't that beat all."

"Flaming jealous."

"Good. And, Ginny?" Colt pulled her up close and rested his nose against hers. "We will always have Paris."

"Uh…what?"

"It just seemed like the right thing to say, us standing here in the dark and the mist, in front of the plane and everything."

"But, we've never been to Paris together."

"It's a turn of phrase, okay? Don't you ever watch old movies? Criminy, how many years will it be before you loosen up?"

Ginny grinned. "A lifetime?"

Colt sighed and buried his nose in her neck. "Deal. And for our honeymoon? Vegas just happens to have a little Paris."

Ginny wrapped her arms around his neck and kissed his lips. "Then," she whispered, "we'll always have Paris."

* * * * *

So, does Carolina end up happily married
to Brandon—or is there someone new
on the horizon? Watch for the next installment of
THE BRUBAKER BRIDES *series,*
next month in Carolyn Zane's
CAROLINA GOES A' COURTING
from Silhouette Romance.

SILHOUETTE *Romance*®

Don't miss

SHARON DE VITA's

exciting new Silhouette Romance title

My Fair Maggy

(Silhouette Romance #1735)

Can a no-nonsense tomboy transform herself into a celebrated advice columnist? Maybe...with the help of soon-to-be retired guidance guru Aunt Millie. But when Millie's nephew takes a shine to the beautiful adviser-in-training, he might need advice on how to win *her* heart....

Available September 2004 at your favorite retail outlet.